Dedication

To George and Gloria Berlow,
also known as Ma and Dad.

Acknowledgments

Continued thanks to
Larry Hammer and Dixie McGuire
for the stories and their support.

"For nothing is secret, that shall not be made manifest; neither any thing hid, that shall not be known and come abroad."

~Luke 8:17, The Bible, King James Version

Part One

Family Reunions

Chapter One

Ever since she was used as a shield by the late Jake Hickey, Miss Elizabeth Handy didn't quite fancy being the wife of a policeman. She may have still had her youthful crush on me but she no longer considered being my spouse as the best option for her. To be perfectly honest, I wasn't at all upset by it. A ghost from the past returned in a vicious way and turned my quiet world on its ear. At this point I knew there was nothing I could give her to make for a long and joyful life. She deserved better. I deserved what I got.

Beth took Frank Appleby up on his proposal of marriage a scant four months after they became a regular item in the local newspaper's "Around Town" column. Truth be told it was really nothing more than gossip from a few cackling ladies who were privy to all the goings-on, casually mentioning it to Sandy Clevenger, the *Arkansas City Traveler's* long-time secretary, who would put her meager literary skills to use. Sandy enjoyed discussing Black Mask stories with me and fancied herself an amateur sleuth. I indulged her because her extensive knowledge on just about everything relating to the city had been invaluable to me. Beth actually broke the news to me even before asking Janet Vogel to be her maid of honor.

"You don't mind, do you, Baron?"

I smiled at her like a big brother would, beaming

with pride.

"Mind? I'm happy for you, Beth. Frank is a good man."

I wasn't much for speeches or philosophical insights. It was all she really needed to hear.

I was fairly confident Dr. Louis Brenz, Doctie as he was known to so many, might have been the only one who knew I was Eric Kimble from the North Side of Chicago and not the beloved Baron Witherspoon from right here in Arkansas City. There was nothing to fear because he was only interested in what was best for the people of Ark City. Besides, what I had become was the type of Baron Witherspoon this city needed, a beat cop with compassion and caring and a no-nonsense attitude. Nothing more. Doctie felt his primary job was to attend to his patients' well-being. To that end, my regular checkups with him were more about the physical, such as the scarring on my face, than anything to do with my mind. He'd tried awful hard to get me right in the head using his training in osteopathy. He figured he was responsible for me seeing as how he brought me into this world. I still had the dreams, probably always would. It was all part of the bargain of being Baron Witherspoon.

Councilman Hallett dropped his title when he declined to run for re-election. If I were a betting man, I would have put the finger on him for most of the graft and corruption in the city. Seeing as how he hadn't been convicted of anything much less charged, his departure from public service was to be considered a victory. I always pegged him for orchestrating Heather Devore's murder in hopes of pinning it on Jake Hickey. Well, Hickey was dead, and the scuttlebutt was Hallett had been "encouraged" to retire by forces more powerful than he had ever dared to be. At this point, it felt like a storm had passed and there was no need to worry about the next one until it arrived. It was something Big Ray Vernon wasn't about to wait for. His long-time dream of being a cop didn't settle too well with the notion of being scared of just about everything. The high school hired him as a history teacher just so he could be assistant coach of the basketball team. I never did quite thank him enough for putting an end to Jake Hickey. I guess me not talking him out of leaving the force was thanks enough.

Most of the town was abuzz over the wedding. It seems like vagrants and ornery young men kept themselves in check for a bit while the festivities were being planned. I knew I would be invited, not because I saved Beth and her dad so much as being an old friend. Even so, a thought crossed my mind I might be out of place, my facial scars not the best thing to present to folks at an occasion which celebrated beauty. I often thought I had a pinkish white spider web hiding everything that could identify me as a human being. Such were the results of struggling in barbed wire in the war. Then I had to be reminded by Mrs. Handy herself I was basically one of the family. It choked me up more than she realized.

The First Baptist Church was a simply stated brick building constructed in 1927, a little less than eight years ago. The Handys had been attending well before then; it was their faith that got them through the most difficult times in their lives, one of which involved me. I still felt awkward being there. It was hard enough coming to grips with being the "new" Baron

Witherspoon I hadn't considered any kind of relationship with my maker. It had never been much of a subject of conversation for tough Irish kids on the North Side of Chicago, despite Dion O'Banion being a churchgoing kind of guy himself. Always wondered what his final reward turned out to be.

On the day of the wedding, I stood at the back just inside the vestibule. The sermon was stuff about loving and honoring and cherishing, all of which I felt Frank Appleby was more than capable.

As the service ended, a rather tall young woman assisted Beth with her train. She had hair the color of new wheat as the sunset shines through it. I don't know why I hadn't seen her earlier. She appeared dipped in gold. I was smiling at Beth and Frank's happiness as the woman passed. Our eyes met briefly. My heart skipped a beat, and I felt kind of breathless. An entirely new sensation for me.

The reception was held at Mr. and Mrs. Appleby's home on account of them having much more room and more land. While Mr. Handy's haberdashery was quite successful, Mr. Appleby was the bank vice-president. They could afford to feed the entire town which is practically what they did. Tables and benches were set up in and around the barn. Fried chicken with all the trimmings turned it into a festive affair. Several boys showed off their yo-yo skills while a couple of girls were chasing a boy rolling an inner tube around with a stick. Nothing stronger than lemonade was served. A few older gentlemen, along with Mr. Appleby, talked politics or business or whatever serious subjects were on their mind. Meanwhile Mr. Handy discussed hats with a few of the wives. Everyone wore their Sunday best. My shirt and tie felt tight around my neck, kind of like a noose. I wasn't used to dressing up so fancy.

The golden-haired woman stood by Beth's side along with the other bridesmaids and wedding party in a reception line. I made my way slowly toward them, head hanging down like a schoolboy. I almost didn't want to look up knowing I would probably say something stupid. Strange how I could look straight into the eyes of the likes of Jake Hickey but a sweet young woman got me to shaking. I was more like Baron Witherspoon now.

I shook Frank's hand firmly and gave him a pat on the arm. Beth reached toward me for a warm hug. She had a small tear in her eye. I wondered if it was because of the day or what I had done for her. I was still looking at her when she said, "Baron, this is my cousin, Natalie Dixon." Because of the introduction, I was forced to look directly at her. She looked back at me without a sliver of fear or apprehension. Her green eyes sparkled like precious jewels. I held her hand lightly.

"I've heard so much about you, Officer Witherspoon." Her tone was gracious and inviting.

"No need to stand on ceremony. You can call me Baron." There was an awkward pause as I could tell she was the type to stand on ceremony. "You don't live around here, do you?"

"I live in Emporia. Went to school up there many years ago. I'm a teacher now."

"That sounds nice." As I figured, it was a dumb thing to say. Meaningless words to fill in the space. Outside of a few gals I had a few drinks and a few laughs with, I had never been around such a genteel woman as Natalie Dixon. I hoped I'd have another chance to speak more intelligently with her if I could figure out how.

I walked to the table with all the food and was so close to grabbing a drumstick when Lee Jones came toward me with strong strides. He was in his mid-twenties and had been on the force about six months. Like many of the new guys, he was eager but largely unprepared for the kind of violence we'd experienced just last year. He would probably do well with drunks and hobos.

"Chief sent me for you." He was panting, out of breath, with sweat pouring down his rather pale face.

"What for?"

"There's something—Well, he said he would tell you."

Lee acted like he'd seen a ghost. I knew not to press him because Chief Richardson was a tall and mean looking man who knew how to impress the younger guys with his demeanor. I made a few quick apologies and left, disappointed about not getting any of Mrs. Appleby's chicken.

Lee's pace was more eager than mine. We made the twenty-minute walk back to the station in ten. I knocked lightly, went into the Chief's office, and stood at attention. I wasn't sure if Chief Richardson had been in the military but knew you always had to follow protocol around this man.

"Mr. and Mrs. Armstrong came across something on the county road as they were driving into church this morning." He started right in without any kind of introduction to the situation. "They came in and reported it and I sent Morton and Jones out to look into it."

It sounded like some kind of campfire story, so mysterious and without any detail. Based on the look on Lee Jones' face, I figured it was no story.

"Morton sent the kid back. I need you to go out there and handle this."

"Why me, sir?" The whole thing had me confused, especially not knowing what the situation actually was. Chief Richardson looked directly at me much in the same way my sergeant did back in France when the situation was dire.

"You've got the kind of intelligence needed for this. The way you handled the Hickey thing proves you're what I need. We've only got but one plainclothesman, and he's not—well, he's not you."

All I could do was say, "Yes, sir" and go with Lee Jones to a lonely county road where Dave Morton had been waiting.

Chapter Two

I truly felt bad for Dave Morton. By the time I got out there, I figure he had been standing on a dusty county road for about an hour in the heat. But he knew Lee wasn't going to be very comfortable just waiting around and wondering what was underneath a bloody sheet.

"How's the shoulder?" I asked, referencing the bullet wound he got from the late Jake Hickey. Dave was a good ten years younger than me but had the kind of maturity the newer guys lacked. I guess part of that came from getting shot by a Chicago gangster.

"It's really cutting into my tennis game," he said with a smile. After fellow officer George McAllister had betrayed us to Hickey by helping him escape, Dave Morton was the one cop I trusted completely. He had smarts and gumption. Reminded me a lot of a younger me. "How was the wedding?"

"Just fine, as far as weddings go. Unfortunately, Lee came to get me right as I was about to eat."

"The Handys like you. I'm sure they'll save you something."

I looked at the road where a clump lay just off to the side. It was covered with a white sheet and had reddish brown stains on it, most likely dried blood.

"What's the story?"

"Don't know."

"What do you mean?"

"The Armstrongs told us what they'd seen and the chief sent us out here. When Lee and I got here, I figured we'd need more people, a doctor maybe."

I looked down at the clump, then to Dave, and back to Lee.

"Anybody look at it?" Dave and Lee both nodded negatively. I knew this is what the chief was referring to.

I leaned down and pulled the sheet back. It was the body of a man who looked like he had run into several of Max Baer's jabs. The right side of the head was swollen and there was a large spot of dried blood. It was clumpy and matted down the hair. Looked like the man had been beaten by some kind of club. Lee viewed the body curiously and, surprisingly, without any sense of disgust.

"That's Carl Bottomley," he blurted out. "He's a bit of a mutt." I wasn't aware of the expression as it related to a human being. Lee saw my furrowed brow and understood my confusion. "His wife and kids left him a long time ago. I'm the same age as his oldest boy. He works at the mill and kind of just goes on about by himself."

I continued pulling the sheet down and saw his body had maybe ten or so stab wounds in the chest and belly. I hadn't seen anything as gruesome since the war. These didn't appear as deep as bayonets but they were sharp.

"How you figure a guy gets killed so violently?" Dave said out loud exactly what I was just thinking. A loner like Lee described would not be a likely victim, certainly not if he didn't get out much.

The sheet had far more blood stains toward the bottom so I kept removing it. What I saw next was something I couldn't prepare for even if you had told me in advance.

His pants had been removed and it appeared his private parts had been cut off. The ground underneath was stained deeper than the red clay of Oklahoma. He was pretty much lying in a pool of blood. I wasn't sure how much the human body contained but by the pale look of his face I figured it had all pretty much just run out.

I had to maintain my composure. Based on my experience, the younger cops believed in me and trusted me because I could keep calm and stay organized. Dave was already aware of how I could handle a situation having dealt with the late 'Crazy' Jake Hickey. This was not the time to vomit in the middle of the street because I had seen something so atrocious.

I turned to Lee, speaking firmly and without a quiver in my voice.

"Lee, I need you to get back to the station. Tell the Chief we need a couple more guys to safeguard the area, an ambulance, and Dr. Brenz. He's at the wedding reception. Tell him we've got an important case but don't say anything else. Don't want to get anyone upset. And make it fast."

Lee nodded and drove off quickly.

"What's this all about, Baron?" Dave was a good cop and a smart man, but he had the same confused look on his face as I did on mine. It was one thing to have gangsters roaming around and corrupt politicians dipping into the till. This was something none us had ever seen. While I appreciated the chief's belief in me, I had no idea how to begin. I looked down at the body covered with so many stab wounds. The smell of decay reminded me of France and the war. The air was thick with heat. Strangely, there weren't any buzzards waiting for a meal. I couldn't see a house or farmstead in any direction. The first thing to figure was how Carl Bottomley got out here.

"He was attacked, and it was a surprise," I blurted out.

"A surprise out here?"

"Just the hit to the head." Dave was squinting his eyes like the sun was blaring in them, and his head was cocked to one side. I leaned down and pointed to the head wound. "It's on the right-hand side, toward the back." I stood up and pretended to be Babe Ruth and then Jimmie Foxx. "The person that hit him was right handed."

"Well, ok, if he got hit from the back. What if he got hit from the front?"

"Wouldn't you see a guy standing in front of you with a club trying to hit you?"

"Yeah, but how do you surprise someone out here?"

It might have been the wrong word to use but I felt the hit to the head was more sudden as opposed to a person being out in the middle of nowhere with Carl. When you're thinking too fast the words don't always come out right. Then again, I wasn't really sure what I was doing or saying.

"You surprise someone by being the kind of person you don't expect to hit you in the head."

"A friend?" Dave's questions were drawing out my thoughts, making me work on answers that didn't previously exist.

"Someone he trusted."

"So, they drive out here," Dave continues, picking up the slack like he's carrying a bucket in a fire brigade, "for some unknown reason. And they get out and Carl walks around aimlessly because he doesn't think anything of this guy. Now, while his back is turned, the guy whacks him on the head, and he drops."

I kept looking at the body, the road, Dave, back and forth, looking for something to come out of the clouds that wasn't just rain. I was sweating like a farmer pitching hay bales, but my thoughts were the only heavy lifting. Talking out a situation wasn't something I was used to doing. Neither was this body before us. At the moment, there was no doctor, no ambulance, no one else who had any experience with this type of crime. It was just Dave and myself who had worked to take out a vicious gangster from Chicago and withstand the workings of corrupt politicians and businessmen.

"Lee said he kept to himself. Who would he have trusted to come out here with?" It was the part didn't make sense. Then again, getting bashed on the head, stabbed nearly a dozen times, and having your wiener cut off didn't make any sense either. I had been a cop since the early 1920s and had never encountered or even read about anything like this. I realized the person who did this was probably a madman and hoped the notion might make it easier to find them.

It must have been an hour by the time Lee drove back with Dr. Brenz, an ambulance, and a car with two other policemen. Dr. Brenz went directly over to the body and grimaced as he looked over the remains.

"Quite a mess," he said matter-of-factly.

"You ever see anything like that, Doctie?" Being considerably older than me, I figured this was something he might have had tucked away in his memory. All he did was shake his head slightly before motioning to the attendants to load the corpse.

"I'll ride with them back to the station," Dave said. "I can give the doc all the info he needs. Besides, the chief will probably want to see you."

I turned to the two patrolmen. "I need you men to visit every farmhouse within the area and ask the residents if they've seen Carl Bottomley recently, up to and including today." They nodded at my command which felt odd to me. I drove back to the station with Lee. Neither one of us said a single word.

Chapter Three

This was one Sunday Chief Richardson was not spending quietly at home with his wife.

"What have you got?"

It seemed as though he thought I had solved a brutal murder in the span of an afternoon. While I appreciated his admiration for what intelligence he thought I had, I wasn't feeling all too smart. I was torn between being frustrated at disappointing him and upset he was expecting too much from me.

"Victim is Carl Bottomley, a mill worker. He was hit on the head, probably to knock him out, then stabbed nearly a dozen times. And then..." The words got stuck in my throat. I had never had to describe anything this brutal before and certainly not to a man in such a position of authority. The chief just looked at me blankly. His eyes blinked a few times while he stood patiently, willing to give me a few more moments before demanding I speak. "His male organs appear to have been sliced off."

"Interesting." It was a little upsetting after all I had just gone through to give me such a minimal response. "Your early thoughts?"

"He went out there with someone he knew or trusted, at least enough to drop his guard while he got smacked. Everything after that shows a lot of anger."

"You ever consider it was the work of a lunatic?"

It was the first thought anyone would have about such a violent killing. It was an easy answer, almost too easy. I couldn't disagree with the notion but the planning it took to lure someone to a remote spot and then attack them was something that went beyond an insane person. Of course, I didn't have the training Dr. Brenz had; I figured more answers would come after a complete exam. As of now, the chief cut me loose for the remainder of the day but instructed me to follow up immediately after the autopsy. I wasn't sure exactly what I was supposed to do from there.

By now, my brain was starting to feel woozy on account of being overly hungry. I got Lee to drive me out to the Appleby home and found the tables and chairs had been brought in. There was nothing wrong with heading down to Daisy Mae's but I had my heart set on Mrs. Appleby's fried chicken.

Sure enough, like a prayer being answered, Natalie Dixon walked out with a brown paper sack in her hand and a small box in the other. She had the accepting smile teachers give to schoolboys who had finished their lessons.

"Mrs. Appleby told me to be on the lookout for you. There's some fried chicken in the sack and a piece of her apple pie in the box." She handed them to me like a priest doling out communion. I felt blessed in more than one fashion.

"She's always been kind to me in that way." I held the sack and the box as though they were ancient treasures. Words escaped me once again. A huge smile overtook my face, and I prayed this would be sufficient to show my feelings, even though I wasn't sure what they actually were.

"Would you…?" she started but couldn't finish any more than I could even speak.

"Yes?" My heart filled in the blanks. Take a walk sometime? Meet for tea at the Handy's house? Visit sometime in Emporia?

"Perhaps you would like to go fishing. I remember this spot by the river where I used to go as a young girl. I hate to go by myself. And, well, it would certainly bring back fond memories."

I certainly wasn't going to tell her fishing absolutely bored me to tears. I didn't tell Big Ray Vernon, and he wasn't half as adorable as Miss Dixon. Besides, it wasn't proper for a young lady to invite a man out on a social occasion. If I wanted to see her again, spend any time around her, I would have to accept.

Dr. Brenz had told me he was working on the autopsy full time now, clearing the appointments he had with his living patients, myself included. This was not the kind of death that could be glossed over in a simple report. I appreciated his attention to detail. More importantly, I appreciated having the time to go on an outing with a charming young lady. In a brief time, she had taken my mind off the most ghoulish thing I had ever encountered. Considering the dreadful war, the barbed wire and the mustard gas, it was saying an awful lot.

Mrs. McGuire, my landlady, was kind enough to make some ham sandwiches for me to bring as a kind of picnic, telling me it would be impolite to let a young lady go hungry. I noticed she was moving about slower and seemed a little unsteady on her feet. She didn't answer me completely when I inquired as to her health, only reassuring me her sister, Miss Bannister, was coming down from Wichita, to help her out. I don't remember my mother Mrs. Kimble much and Mrs. Witherspoon wasn't in my life all too long. I had the kind of concern for Mrs. McGuire a son would have. I just didn't have enough experience to know what to do about it.

Natalie Dixon appeared quite a natural putting a worm on her hook and casting a line into the water. I was still rather awkward, and she was quite amused at my clumsiness. Getting a hook caught in my thumb was painful for me but a source of mild amusement for her. I didn't mind too much because I realized I felt more relaxed around her than any other girl I had known.

I laid a blanket down by the edge of the river so we could have our sandwiches without her getting soiled. The whole afternoon was making me feel gallant, like a gentleman or a knight in armor in days of castles and courts. I didn't feel like a country boy from the farms of Kansas but I also didn't feel like a street punk from Chicago.

"What was it like, in the war I mean?" She asked like a teacher would, as though she were trying to learn something she could pass on to others.

I paused for a bit before answering. The war had changed my life completely, but I tried desperately not to think of it regularly.

"Scary, most of the time. The bullets and the shells all over the place. You couldn't tell who was shooting at who. All the smoke felt like fire and brimstone in Hell." I didn't want to just leave it at the bad part. There was Baron Witherspoon who became my closest friend and showed me how I could live my life if I chose, with a little more decency and consideration. When he died, I honored him by living that way. "I really had no idea what is was all about, you know, the politicians and the governments. But the guys with you, in the trenches, running alongside you, is what you fought for. You fought for them."

As I figured, I didn't catch a thing. She threw back two crappies and a small catfish. Maybe she was saving me the further embarrassment of cleaning them. We walked back to town barefoot like we didn't have a care in the world.

"I'd sure like to see you again, Natalie. You're, well, just so easy to be around."

"Are you asking me out on a date, Officer Witherspoon?"

I smiled. I guess I was asking her out on a date.

Chapter Four

I was in the records room going through every homicide for the past twenty-years. It was an unused office, practically a closet with one uncomfortable wooden chair and a table with warbling legs. It wasn't a place you would spend a great deal of time. I didn't think there would be as many cases as, let's say, Chicago. But this sleepy little village less than ten miles from the Oklahoma border had a record of killings of mostly robbers and gangsters fighting each other over valuable territory, especially when liquor was illegal and every home had a still. Charles Floyd was known as Choc by the Okies; he was "Pretty Boy" to the Feds. Folks around these parts thought of him as a modern-day Robin Hood. The papers said he was a vicious killer. Everyone was bound to remember him just a little different.

Nothing I was able to dig up pointed to anything as heinous as what we found out on a county road east of town. From all I was able to discover about Carl Bottomley, he wasn't a drinker or a gambler and wasn't in debt to anyone. Yet, this crime was committed with such violence and anger I was sure there had to be something about him to trigger such a harsh response.

Providing all these details to Chief Richardson, I was calm and collected. For whatever reason he entrusted me to investigate this murder, I knew I couldn't undermine his faith in me. I was surprised to see him showing just the slightest bit of emotion, swallowing hard or squinting at the details. This big, heavy-set man seemed resistant to just about anything. I had just discovered his weak spot.

It sounded like Anthony Downs race track right outside the door with two thoroughbreds clambering for position along the pole. Screeching to a halt and throwing open the door was Lee Jones and his boyhood friend and fellow officer, Jay Davis. From the galloping sounds, you would have thought they had been running all over the place looking for me. Come to find out they were. Even though their uniforms were brand new, they both looked rumpled. They were probably more used to overalls and t-shirts.

"Hey, Baron, me and Jay were talking…"

"Yeah, we were talking about Carl Bottomley. We knew his oldest boy."

"I told him that."

"But you didn't tell him…"

"I was going to."

I felt like I was watching a couple of baggy pants comedians in a burlesque show. I whistled as loud as I could to get their attention. They stopped and turned to look at me simultaneously, both with their eyes bugging out. Either they didn't notice they just barged into the chief's office or were too scared to let on they knew. "One at a time," I said with enough force to sound like the commissioner. "Jay. Go ahead."

"We both knew Bottomley's oldest son. Went to school with him. His mom took him and his younger brother and just left town, up and skedaddled about ten years ago."

Lee felt compelled to interject. "Twelve. It was twelve years ago because we were just going into high school."

"Why did she leave?" It seemed an appropriate question to ask.

"Couldn't say," Lee continued. "I asked my mom at the time about it. All she said was Mrs. Bottomley had to."

It was more than I had before but not enough to make sense. I couldn't see Mrs. Bottomley returning to get revenge for an unspecified reason. I didn't know the lady but this didn't appear to be the work of a woman. On the other hand, either of the two sons might have wanted to avenge their mother if they felt she had been slighted in any way.

"I need you two to talk to anyone who knew the Bottomleys, not just Carl but the entire family. Other school mates. Teachers who still might be at the school. We need to find out why she left town and where they are now. All of them."

Chief Richardson hadn't said anything during this exchange. He was giving me enough room to show authority. He would step in when it was necessary.

I needed to break away for a bit and get my head together. I kept seeing a bloody corpse under a sheet by the side of a road. It was so unlike the uniformed soldiers in dark and misty French forests. The sheet covering the body was yet another source of confusion, as though the killer had some kind of regret. It was an opportune time to go to the motion pictures with Natalie. She mentioned there a showing of *A Midsummer Night's Dream*, and just like with fishing, I didn't have the heart to tell her I wasn't the world's biggest fan of Shakespeare. When it turned out *Mutiny on the Bounty* was playing instead, the pout on her face was endearing but I wasn't going to make her suffer through a man's story about sailors on the high seas. We chose instead to just go for a walk.

She asked me more about the war and how I was able to get through the hard times and how difficult it was to get back to this life. Her voice was just above a whisper, soft like a feather on my ears. It was funny how, for so many years, I tried to let it all go with Dr. Brenz's help and now she was bringing me back to it. Truth was I didn't mind with her. Somehow I felt she could relate to me though I never knew how. What pleased me the most was how she looked at me, directly, eye to eye, never blinking or looking away in disgust, like she wanted to really see me as a person, a real human being behind the deeply etched lines in my face. It was a little scary considering I wasn't sure who she was actually seeing.

"It's important to move on and it's good you're trying." I don't recall any of my teachers from Lincoln Park. The closest she sounded was how I imagined Mrs. McGuire might have sounded at Natalie's age. "I think too many people let the past creep into their dreams and hold them hostage, not letting them move on. What good is that? You might as well die right there on the spot."

"I don't know what would have happened if I had. I don't think about it much. Heck, I hadn't thought of it at all until you mentioned it. I suppose there are so many roads a person can go down."

"You need to keep walking down your road, Baron, wherever it may lead, and don't let anyone stop you. Don't let anything hold you back."

She sounded like Doctie, seeming to know something she couldn't possibly know. But it was more than that, almost as though she could empathize in a real and personal way even though she had never been haunted by war.

The thing which haunted me now was Carl Bottomley. Less than two weeks later Thomas Sutton was added to that nightmare.

Chapter Five

It was rather disturbing to consider this body was several hundred yards from where I had been fishing with Natalie. The condition of the corpse upon discovery was fresh so it wasn't there when we were. One of the other patrol officers found Sutton covered with dead leaves and branches. It had the same markings and mutilation as Carl Bottomley. We found a heavy stone with blood stains and determined it to be the cause of the crushed skull. There were stab marks on his back and his genitals had been cut off, but he was found lying on his stomach. Since he was a larger, heavy-set man, it would have taken a certain amount of effort.

There was a file on Tom Sutton back at the municipal station. Seems as though he had been brought in on several Drunk and Disorderly violations a few years ago and then his record had a gap until just the last few months. The latest arrest identified him as working at the Shell refinery. I could count on getting info on him from Larry Hammer, the chief maintenance man out there. Larry knew just about everyone in town but made sure to stay out of their business. It was one of the many things that made him useful to me. I knew I would find him propped up on a stool at Daisy Mae's.

The apple pie was so fresh you could see the steam rise as you walked in and smell something like an autumn afternoon. Larry didn't have the patience to eat slowly. He claimed it was his way of letting Dixie know how good her food was. It sure was important if you wanted to stay in her good graces. Truth was he always felt like he had to rush off to some place or another. Didn't want any moss growing under his feet.

"Hey, Baron." No matter how much of a rush he felt he was under, he always had time for me. I gave him the kind of respect his bosses never thought to give.

"You know a Tom Sutton? I believe he works out at Shell."

A solid set of nods was followed by "I've seen him around. Doesn't have much good to say about anyone."

"No friends?"

"None around now."

Larry knew him back when, said he had a mean disposition, then up and disappeared, although there was some talk he did a stretch down in McAlester but was uncertain for what. The current bosses at Shell were not the same ones from ten plus years ago so he got hired back on since he did have some skills. Larry felt Sutton was just too loud to fit in with the rest of the guys despite his abilities and figured it was a matter of time before he'd wind up in trouble again. However, neither Larry nor anyone else would have thought he'd get his brains bashed in and his balls cut off.

When I got back to the station, Chief Richardson was standing outside his office looking like he had got stood up on a date. He was waiting for me. I got a funny feeling, like a big stone in the pit of my stomach. I was getting frustrated but the chief was fit to be tied. He closed the office door and drew the blinds. His tone was forceful, like a locomotive rumbling through a station, but it was controlled.

"I need to know where you're at with this, Witherspoon."

"I've got nothing, sir. Best I can figure is something in these men's pasts. Bottomley's wife and kids left him twelve years ago. It coincides with the approximate time Thomas Sutton left town. Apparently both these men had their secrets."

"Is it revenge?"

"Looks more like justice." I knew as soon as I spoke it was the wrong word to use. It was the thing that struck me the most about these two horrific deaths especially after hearing stories about these victims. Arkansas City, Kansas had not experienced this kind of brutality at least since I became a cop. I didn't know much about madmen and lunatics, despite the brief lesson Dr. Brenz tried to give me. It just appeared like someone had tried these men in their own mind and felt this was a righteous punishment.

"We've got our own justice in this town, Officer Witherspoon." Maybe the chief was in agreement with me but didn't find it proper to say so as clearly. "If this does have something to do with their past, perhaps you better get up to Winfield and see what you can find out."

The Cowley County Courthouse is where trials for major crimes would have taken place. Whatever records we had in the city would have been minimal, arrest records and citations. It was getting too late in the day to drive up. An early start would be more ideal.

I was squirming inside because I remembered I promised to take Natalie to dinner. There was something happening between us I felt could grow if we just gave it a chance. Casual conversations and walks and a lot of looking into each other's eyes was the stuff in books women read. But she was able to reach inside me and touch something I felt had been dead for so long. Perhaps she is what Eric Kimble had been looking for back as a teenager in Chicago. In any case, I knew I needed to see her and make certain she had the same feeling for me. I was pushing forty and finally feeling like my life was amounting to more than just walking a beat. I would have walked anywhere if I knew she'd be by my side.

She had been staying with Beth ever since the wedding. It was rather awkward calling on the phone what with me not showing any interest in Beth for all those years and now asking for her cousin. I just wasn't aware how much the whole thing with Jake Hickey had made Mrs. Elizabeth Appleby grow up.

"You don't think I forgot you?" I was sounding coy on purpose. Imagine that.

"I was beginning to think so."

"I've got to get on up to the county courthouse tomorrow for a case. But I'd still like to take you to dinner. You know, if you want to go." It was then I realized I wasn't playing at being shy. I really felt that way. Staring down a gun, either with gangsters or German soldiers, was nothing compared to someone who makes you realize who you really are.

I knew right then I was going to work real hard on this case and then work harder on trying to make some kind of life for me and Natalie Dixon. I couldn't tell if I was thinking about quitting the force or just making a leap of faith. Maybe I was being foolish, but I was a fool with a big smile on my face. I hadn't realized how this case was going to make it difficult for me to keep smiling.

Chapter Six

You don't really realize how poor your manners are until you sit down with someone who has them. Any time me and the guys, Lee and Jay or Dave, would get down to Daisy Mae's, we would shovel Dixie's burgers into our pie hole faster than a jackrabbit chasing a mouse. Sitting opposite Natalie, I felt myself rushing through the meal as though I were trying to get to a fire. It wasn't even my line of work.

Tony's Inn was a fancy name for an Italian restaurant owned by Anthony Calicchio. He had traditional food like spaghetti and ravioli, but also made sure to have steaks on the menu for those who were not so inclined to have sauce on everything. Tony was a few years older than me and his place was known for red and white checkerboard tablecloths and real candles on the table. I wasn't the romantic type. This was the closest I could get, and Anthony helped me make it special.

Natalie didn't make funny noises like Jay when she ate her spaghetti. In fact, she twirled it on her fork until it was a small mound and then bit daintily into it. I made sure to chew the meatballs well so I wouldn't wind up talking with my mouth full. I felt like a young boy in church minding my Ps and Qs.

"This is very nice," she said softly. "Have you been here before?"

"Once." Since it was a rather romantic place, I added, "But not with anyone else. I mean, I—"

"Don't worry. I'm not the jealous type."

I was having a hard time trying to relax and just sit back. I slumped over my plate like Lon Chaney in *The Hunchback of Notre Dame,* sopping up sauce with my garlic bread. I hoped I wasn't grunting at the time. I was rushing through, hurrying to finish up when Natalie reached across the table and touched my hand. Our eyes met. I allowed a small smile to emerge, and I nodded my head slightly.

Tony himself removed the plates from the table. I cleared my throat perhaps a little too loudly. If I didn't know better, I would have sworn I was going to propose.

"I've never thought about my future much before." My voice was a tad above a whisper. Even if I knew what I was going to say, I would have still felt my heart beating through my chest, trying its darnedest to get out. "Being around you though has made me—"

"Think about your future?" I couldn't tell if she was teasing me or helping me get the darned words out from being stuck in my teeth. "I felt the same way, too," she continued, allowing me to sigh in relief. "Sometimes you get to where you wonder what your purpose in life is, what you're supposed to be doing. It took me a while but I discovered it."

"Teaching," I said confidently.

She paused briefly, looking directly at me with a very serious look on her face, eyes focused, lips pursed. "Yes."

I took it to mean her career was all that meant anything to her. After all, she was in her early thirties and would have been married by now if she wanted. I remember growing up and all the teachers looked old. Then again, thirty might have been old to a six-year-old. The teachers I had known in Ark City were either young enough to be looking for a husband or too old to even care about having one. Natalie might have been at the tipping point, trying to decide what to do. I was hoping I was a part of the decision.

Since I had a long day ahead of me, I felt like it was getting late but I didn't want to let her go, didn't want anything left unsaid either of us needed to say. My mind and attention were going to be focused on something completely opposite of what was happening at this table. I needed the memory of this to get me through. It was just a bit cool yet pleasant enough for a stroll. There was no place to go but we were going there anyway.

"Do you suppose I could see you again, Natalie?"

"For as long as I'm here, Baron."

"So, you're not staying long?"

"I only came down for, well, Elizabeth's wedding. I've got to get back to Emporia, to the school."

"I heard they need a third-grade teacher at Adams elementary." Knowing her leaving was a possibility, I made some inquiries from a couple of the local school principals hoping to make this the best possible place to settle down.

She smiled. I felt like a young kid who had a crush on his teacher. Then I remembered I used to be Eric Kimble, a tough little Irish kid from the streets of Chicago who went off to fight the Hun in Europe and came back as the scarred Baron Witherspoon. It was time to shake off the dust of this foolish dandy I had allowed myself to become. The boy had become a man. I needed to start acting that way.

"Natalie, you've become something very special to me. I've never said that about any woman before. You make me understand myself more clearly than I ever felt. I was hoping, well, I still hope there's a place for me in your life. I think we would do well by each other."

She reached up and touched my face with her hand, gently and softly, her forefinger touching against my deepest scars, without fear or concern. She was a teacher and a kind soul. She embraced my defects as though they were strengths.

"I didn't think any man could touch me the way you have. I know you're hiding in there, behind those scars. And I know you must feel lonely. Believe me, I am, too. But I can't give myself to you. I can't give myself to anyone. There's far too much sadness in me, and I don't want anyone to have to carry that burden."

Her hand practically fell to her side. I reached for it, held it dearly, and then walked her back to the car and drove her home in silence. She stepped out of the car and strode toward the front door of the Appleby's house. I didn't quite know what troubles she had within her but I felt as though I would probably never see her again. It saddened me knowing I had lost my best chance for anything other men called Love. At the very least, I got to experience something I had never felt before. Now the Light was to be snuffed by the Darkness.

Chapter Seven

I got up early and found Miss Banister, Mrs. McGuire's sister, had some hot black coffee waiting for me and a plate of biscuits and gravy. I remember only vaguely mentioning I had an out-of-town appointment so it was surprising to see something hearty on the table. She had a light airy sense to her. Her hand-sewn apron already had flour dusting on it as well as what appeared to be cocoa.

"I have a special dessert, a chocolate zucchini cake, assuming you'll be back in time for dinner." She spoke with an openness and affection.

"How is your sister, ma'am?"

"Resting."

She had a curt smile on her face, her lips tightly pursed, but still with a bit of a twinkle in her eye. Seems both sisters were adept at keeping things hidden. It was my cue to end the trail of conversation.

The sweet young clerk at the courthouse who only last year got to hear the story of how my name became Baron due to a typographical error was still behind her desk and still grinning sweetly, apparently unaware of the criminals surrounding her. She directed me to Officer Elmore who I learned practically lived in the records room in the basement. His freckles made him look younger but there were fine soft lines at the corner of his eyes that showed how much of a reader he was.

"So, what exactly are you looking for?"

"Violent murders in and around Ark City for, say, the past fifteen years."

"Violent?" I showed him a photo of Carl Bottomley and Thomas Sutton as they were found. He nodded with the same kind of appreciation as a friend who had caught a large catfish. "I'd say that was pretty violent."

He escorted me down two flights of stairs. From what I'd read of ancient Rome, these seemed like similar catacombs. Our shoes echoed with hollow clicks and the infinitely long hallway was like a ghost town, something that had outgrown its usefulness. Elmore walked to a door with frosted glass and the simple word "RECORDS" painted on it. The other doors farther down were just wood with no window.

The room I initially entered had a large wooden table, enough for six guys to sit around playing poker. There were floor to ceiling shelves on two sides, one extending only three-quarters of the way, which allowed a hallway between them. This was where the other doors were. Each door opened onto an aisle of file cabinets, four high, five across, on each side of the recessed area where they were located. Tags on each cabinet indicated town or city and year. Eight of these recessed areas stretched down the length of the hallways.

"And if that ain't enough for you, there's an identical set-up on the other side of the corridor." His satisfied smile let me and anyone else know this was his domain. The other cops, the District Attorney, the judges, none of them would even dare to venture down here. You would practically have to tie a rope to yourself to be pulled out if you got lost. Officer Elmore would have his job for as long as he wanted it, and the county would be in dutch once he left. I was figuring I'd have to forego Miss Banister's dessert.

Fortunately, Arkansas City was at the beginning, alphabetically speaking. Unfortunately, it didn't wind up being as much of a help as I thought. Whereas there weren't a whole lot of murders, the violent crimes involved beatings and robberies and a few lynchings I wasn't too especially proud to read. I sat there thinking how it was possible one man could be so cruel to another. Then it dawned on me I grew up in an area where another man's life stood in the way of one's own success. People like Jake Hickey didn't have much in the way of compassion. Of course, I was forgetting, or perhaps trying to forget, the war itself, one the greatest examples of inhumanity that ever existed. It was better for me to just slog my way through this without thinking and judging.

Every once in a while, my mind drifted away from all the black clouds I was reading and wandered to the light that was Natalie. It was such a strange feeling, going from the intensity of figuring out who a vicious killer might be and the warmth that came over me when I was around her. It was a shame I had to snuff the flame momentarily in order to focus on the important police matter.

I made it down it to M towns before I realized several hours had passed and I was hungry. I stumbled out into the hallway, started one way before I realized I was heading for a dead end, and then turned around. My heels clicked on the polished floor and echoed as I imagined it would in some old castle. Officer Elmore must have had the sixth sense of a cat.

"You done?" he asked. I wasn't sure if he was joking or not.

"Just started on Maple City. I was fixing on getting something to eat."

Officer Elmore looked at his watch and started shaking his head with a look of disappointment.

"By the time you get done, my shift will have ended. And there's really no one else that can help. They've kind of left it all to me, if you know what I mean." It would be an awful big effort for me to drive back to Ark City and then come back up in the morning. Elmore was rubbing his chin, sizing me up, probably figuring I was the same kind of paperwork busybody like him. "We got an extra bedroom ever since the kid moved out. The wife wouldn't mind none if I told her she wouldn't."

I spent the majority of the evening listening to Mrs. Elmore reciting episodes of her husband's successes as a policeman prior to his acceptance of this more clerk type position. I got the impression she felt she lost her hero while he was glad to be out of harm's way. Overall, it was gratifying to see such a relationship and wondered if such a possibility could be mine as well.

The next morning after being treated to a sizable breakfast I picked up my efforts where I left off. It didn't take me but a part of the morning to get to an incident involving school children from Parkerfield. It was a small unincorporated burg just east of Ark City. Population was less than a hundred and they were largely farming families. Despite attending school in Arkansas City, the report was filed under the town in which the children lived. Carl Bottomley, Thomas

Sutton, and a third man, Jeremy Collins, had approached a group of ten young girls with their teacher on a picnic outing. The men appeared to be drunk. They grabbed several girls although there was no violation of them. The teacher was slapped around. Several plates were smashed. The men used foul language and threatened the girls, making suggestive and lewd comments. After thirty minutes of this horror, the men basically became bored and left. The teacher quickly gathered the girls and returned to town where the incident was reported. A description of the men was provided. By the end of the evening, all three were apprehended and bound over for trial. The judge either showed more compassion than was required or didn't have any granddaughters to consider because the men received thirty-day prison sentences, largely for the destroyed property.

There was probably not going to be any other reference for the two murdered men but I had to be as thorough as possible. By mid-afternoon, I had gotten all through with Winfield. This report from Parkerfield was the only instance which referenced Bottomley and Sutton. My task now was to locate Collins and see what he knew. I asked Elmore if I could borrow the file. He looked it over, saw the date printed on the front and nodded affirmatively.

"Fifteen years old and two of the men dead. I don't think we'll be needing it anymore." I turned to walk upstairs but he still had his hand on the edge of the folder. "Of course, when you are done with it, I'd like to get it back. You know, just to keep everything in order." I was certain I would be able to accommodate.

Chapter Eight

I was torn between thinking Jeremy Collins was some kind of despicable bum or he was in grave danger. I never gave much thought to considering both might have been true. It wasn't for me to determine his character or worthiness. It is why the system had judges. Protecting and serving the public was the only dictate we were given. Still, I couldn't imagine why a rabble rouser would be the target of someone's vicious vengeance. Seems like all they did was scare a bunch of schoolgirls and use language more fitting for a refinery or a gin mill late on a Saturday night. At the very least, we had two names: a possible target and a spinsterish schoolteacher.

I gathered Dave Morton, Lee Jones, and Jay Davis just outside the chief's office.

"Lee, you and Jay will need to locate a—" I looked down at the file. "—Julia Brayfield. She was a teacher…"

"Mrs. Brayfield," Jay burst out. "She was old when my brother Phil had her."

"Isn't Phil older than you?" I inquired.

"Yep." Lee and Jay knew her well enough to be able to locate her, although she had retired nearly twelve years before, not long after the incident in the file. I took a more sober approach with Dave.

"This Jeremy Collins is the only thing that

connects Carl Bottomley and Tom Sutton. If anyone knows anything, it's him." It was largely speculation on my part but at this point it was all we had. Dave had given the file the once over and was as perplexed as I was.

"I guess you can't really know what happened out there to stir someone up so bad."

"Find him," I said, practically gasping. "We need him."

I had an extended conversation with Chief Richardson. He listened patiently, trying not to appear as frustrated as I was. No one of importance, per se, was breathing down his neck on this one, not like when Mr. Hallett was Councilman Hallett and this sort of thing was bad for business, corrupt or legitimate. It was more like the chief's own sense of personal and professional pride that drove him to getting this thing closed. An unsolved case was one thing. One reeking of violence and hatred would leave a stain on his legacy.

For the next two nights, I sat in an empty office reading medical reports and looking at the photos, hearing Dr. Brenz's voice running through my mind. I was trying to imagine, if I could, what had taken place during these men's death. By putting together a step-by-step story, so to speak, I might be able to consider what kind of man it would take to commit these crimes. Hopefully, I would actually be able to find him.

They had each been hit on the back of the head, presumably to knock them out. That might indicate surprise but they were each found in a remote area. They wouldn't have just been out there meandering about while the madman stalks them like a hunter and hits them on the head. Why would the killer hit the victims from behind? Bottomley and Sutton both must have known or trusted the man, enough to go with him to these areas. The forceful blow did more than surprise them. It incapacitated them.

Bottomley was six foot four inches. Sutton was five foot ten. Each was struck on the right side but closer to their ear. It meant the man was shorter and right-handed. Dr. Brenz counted fourteen stab wounds about Bottomley's neck and chest. Sutton had twelve in his back mostly between the shoulder blades. So after hitting them on their head to knock them down, the man feverishly stabbed them in a fit of anger. But it wasn't the thing that caused their death because no major organs were struck. If it all that had been done, each of the men would have bled to death, most likely in agonizing pain according to Doctie.

Something like a straight razor was used to remove their genitals. In reading this particular section of the report, I kept thinking back to all the blood on the floor of the room in the Gladstone where Heather Devore met her end. Jake Hickey's moll dressed in a negligee and lying in a pool of deep red blood the likes of which I had never seen before. It was a sinister way to die, one she certainly didn't deserve. Someone thought otherwise of Carl Bottomley and Thomas Sutton.

The medical report indicated cause of death was extreme loss of blood. Dr. Brenz figured there was also shock and other trauma. Was that intended or was the killer sloppy? It was hard to determine if making them suffer by bleeding to death was the actual point or if the castration had the greater meaning. I assumed a deep hatred more than a mental illness. It was, after all, something I could relate to from my recent past.

There was a point where I hated Jake Hickey not so much for what he had done in his past but how he was disturbing my life and those of the people around me. I didn't care if the people of Arkansas City, Kansas found out I was Eric Kimble from Chicago instead of their beloved Baron Witherspoon. I was going to kill Hickey. It took a special kind of hatred to bring out such anger. In this regard, I shared something with this man: We were both driven to the furthest point of our anger.

Dave and I reviewed personnel files of the refinery and finally came across a couple of possibilities. Robert Morgan was in his fifties, a former bare-knuckle boxer and had been in and out of jail for minor offenses, mostly fighting when it wasn't in the ring. One skirmish was with Sutton. Nothing came of it. Tim Kruger was in his late sixties, pretty much a drunk with bad teeth and bad breath who was surprisingly still able to hold down a job, and had numerous citations for Disturbing the Peace, Petty Theft, and Discharging a Weapon in the city. He worked with all three at one point or another and had done some work on behalf of the Wobblies shortly after the war. However, it was a stretch to connect labor union activists with murder, and I just couldn't see an old man having the wherewithal to commit these crimes.

There was a mental image of this man, this vicious killer, in my mind. But I could not see him clearly, just a well-built shadow with evil red eyes seeking revenge. Or justice. There was smoke in the trees, and this creature was hiding behind it. I needed a name to attach to this ghostly figure.

While Officer Davis and Officer Jones finally

located Mrs. Brayfield, there was a reason to worry. A niece indicated Mrs. Brayfield was now in the Ponca City Hospital run by the Sisters of St. Joseph. She had cancer and was dying. This would mean another trip, over thirty miles south into Oklahoma. Into the land that bred Wilber Underhill Jr. and Charles Arthur Floyd. I knew the Sisters of St. Joseph would have more compassion. I was hoping Julia Brayfield would live long enough to help me catch a killer.

Chapter Nine

I had seen death before. Countless times. Watched the closest thing I had to a brother, Baron Witherspoon, get blown to bits just after pushing me into a foxhole and saving me by literally landing on top of me. Seen other comrades fall. Was staring in the face of Jake Hickey, 'Crazy' Jake, a madman of a gangster, when Big Ray Vernon shot him in the back of the head. In war and crime, death was expected. But I had not seen the dying. My dad, actually Baron's dad, fell ill from a stroke while I was on patrol. By the time they found me and brought me to the hospital, he had expired. Now, I would be in the presence of a woman whose life was ebbing away. She needed to hold on, just long enough to help our case. I would be there to witness her pain and suffering. Perhaps not all of it was from the cancer.

The sisters spoke as quietly as librarians but their tone was soft and comforting. It was as though they had the kind of voices necessary to walk hand in hand with death. Sister Leary was perhaps in her early sixties with a stern face yet gentle eyes, almost tired. Yet there was nothing that could pull her away from her duties. It was evident she could balance protocol and compassion. She explained to me Mrs. Brayfield had been diagnosed with cancer of the bowels which had progressed too far to warrant an operation. The Ponca City Hospital was providing comfort, both physically and spiritually.

"I have important questions to ask her. It could help solve a case." My voice was almost as gentle as hers.

"We can't afford to upset…"

"She may help us catch a killer." I hated to interrupt a nun. She was the kind to save souls. My job was to save lives. My eyes must have resembled a boy's favorite bloodhound.

"I will be in the room. The interview will cease when I say."

I nodded. It was all I could do.

Julia Brayfield, I was told, was seventy-four years old yet she looked ancient. Her deep-set eyes looked beyond tired, and a blanket of wrinkles made me look like Clark Gable. The illness may have worn her down but I recall Jay and Lee referencing her as looking old years ago. There was a slight tremor in her lips and her eyes were filled with tears. Perhaps she could see her savior and was overjoyed at the thought of stepping over.

In the discussions with Sister Leary, there was never any mention of how my appearance might affect Mrs. Brayfield. Part of me was glad about that. By the same token, I didn't want the dear lady to believe the devil was coming for her.

"Mrs. Brayfield, I'm Officer Baron Witherspoon from Ark City."

Her eyes fluttered as she looked at me. It was as though a haze were clearing.

"I know you."

"Ma'am?"

"The boy who came back from the war."

"Yes, ma'am." I was able to put a smile on my face

for her. It put me at ease perhaps more than her.

"You've done your parents proud."

It was a sentiment I'm sure every schoolteacher has hoped to have.

"Do you recall a time when three men disturbed a school picnic way back?"

Her lips clenched in bitterness. It was still a strong memory.

"Very bad men."

"Yes, ma'am."

She shook her head in defiance. Then tears started to roll gently down her face.

"I was supposed to keep them safe."

"But you did."

"No." She repeated it over and over. "I didn't. They got her. I just know it was them."

"Who? Who did they get, Mrs. Brayfield?"

"Little Kimberly."

Her head was moving from side to side and she was sobbing fully now. She was recalling a failure of some kind but not the events of the picnic. I couldn't continue any further because Sister Leary stepped in right then and pulled me back from the bedside.

I certainly wasn't going to try to make arrangements to come back. It would have been too much for the dear lady to bear. I already hated myself for allowing her to think she did anything less than her best to protect those girls. I was starting to hate those men even more.

At least I had a name. I didn't have the case file with me but it was something. Mrs. Brayfield felt she didn't protect Kimberly, whoever she was. I might have been able to go back to Winfield and visit with my new friend, Officer Elmore, but it could have taken yet another full day. Then it dawned on me I was overlooking one of my favorite resources: Sandy Clevenger from the *Traveler*, the long-time secretary who had all the old editions and knew every bit of history and gossip from the last forty years. Sandy knew anything worthwhile there was to know.

As I drove back, it started to make sense. Kimberly, whoever she was, suffered in some way other than what was listed in the file. I considered she may have had a mental breakdown due to the trauma of the three men. I'm sure she had a father or brother or uncle who was upset at the outcome. After thoroughly going over all the reports and looking at the photos until my eyes were red and feeling burned by the sun, I could not accept the notion of some raving lunatic who killed two men in the most brutal fashion I had ever seen simply out of randomness. Now it was just a matter of identifying Kimberly.

It was late when I got back to Ark City. I had made the mistake of not getting something to eat before I left Oklahoma. There were feelings of remorse for the sufferings of Mrs. Brayfield. I was just plain tired and certainly not prepared to greet Dave Morton at the Municipal Building. He had a look of anticipation. It was actually the face of defeat.

"Well? Did you find Jeremy Collins?"

"Yeah." There was an eerie silence like in a graveyard. "He's with Dr. Brenz."

Chapter Ten

He was laid out on a table in the back room of Dr. Brenz's office. Sheet covering him. Blood stains, red but almost rust colored. Doctie was looking down toward the floor but not at it, shaking his head, surely at the frustration more than the sight of death. Dave had a blank look on his face. He's a smart guy but I could tell he was out of ideas. Never thought I'd ever have something like this fall into my lap and feel utterly useless.

"Same as the others?" I asked.

Dr. Brenz brought his file up and put his glasses on.

"Not quite. There were far more stab wounds than the other two. I counted twenty-six."

Dave was impressed enough to whistle and then realized it might have been considered inappropriate.

"Well, what about major organs?" I continued, recalling the previous medical reports which had been burned into my mind.

"The aorta was punctured and the spleen and liver were severely damaged. Mr. Collins probably died much quicker than the other two, uh, gentlemen."

"What about the—?"

"Yes, well, more crudely done. Something more akin to a steak knife as the edges seemed ragged. Overall, I would speculate the degree of anger was greater than before. The sequence of the assault was the same. However, as it is more than likely Mr. Collins expired quicker, the killer continued his stabbing and proceeded with what appears to be the ultimate act which is, of course, the castration."

Dr. Brenz spoke with the eloquence of a college professor attempting to be as professional and discreet as possible. The long and the short of it was Jeremy Collins was the main target of the three, just by virtue of the excess of stab wounds.

"You think this is going to continue?" Dave's question was relevant but even he could see the overall picture. At this point, if Collins was the primary target and perhaps the final one, our killer was going to slink back under the rock he came from. Our time was limited. The only person I needed to see now was Mrs. Collins.

The walk felt like a forced march in the Army, the steps practically beating into the ground, making my own ruts in the road. Dave was hard pressed to keep up with me. He had never seen me this way. It wasn't a knock on the door like a pastor coming for a visit. I was rattling the walls of the castle, an invader demanding entry. The mouse that answered the door had eyes sunken into her face and skin as pale as death itself. She resembled her late husband even though she was still breathing.

"We need to talk, Mrs. Collins. It's about your husband."

"He didn't do anything," she said while shaking her head as though to dry her hair. "He never did." I didn't wait for her to invite me in. I walked past her, brushing her shoulder with mine. Dave followed and quietly closed the door as Mrs. Collins followed me dutifully.

"What makes you think we're here because he's done something? Has he done something, recently or in the past?" She was talking about guilt without even knowing why we were there much less asking.

"No. Never." I swear her head was going to snap off her neck from the force of her denial.

"That's not true. I've got court records to prove it."

"It was he and his drunk buddies getting out of hand. That's all. They didn't do nothing."

I looked around the house. It was plain and had only what was needed. There was nothing hanging on the wall. Not a cross or a sampler or a photo of the grandparents or children. Nothing. An emptiness as though real flesh and blood people weren't living there but some kind of ghosts making up for their past. For all I knew she was as dead as her husband.

"Jeremy's dead, ma'am. Your husband's dead." Dave had a peaceful way about him when he had a mind for it. Maybe he saw me being too mean or this woman being too innocent. But I was figuring opposite. I was guessing she knew all about her husband, knew what kind of man he was, at least to her and maybe his own kids. I was thinking when everything happened all those years ago and her husband and two drunk buddies were brought up before a judge, she had a good idea exactly what they were up to and what they were meaning to do.

She looked like someone pulled the plug on a cistern and emptied it dry. As pale as she was to begin with, she appeared almost invisible now. We stood there in silence for a long time, just me and Dave and a woman who had stopped being herself for a very long time.

"He was just drunk is all," she finally said, almost whispering. "They all was."

"That's what the judge figured." I wanted to keep her talking. By agreeing with her, I was hoping she'd feel safe. She sat down on the divan, more like fell into it, allowing it to be her confessional.

"They went back afterward."

"Afterward? After what?"

"After the trial. After they done their time. They went back to the school."

"Why?"

"They was mad. Mad at the teacher. They was going to..." She looked up at me hoping I knew what she meant, unable to say it aloud. I nodded for her to continue. "But instead they followed this one girl. Sweet girl she was. Grabbed her and drove her out to the spot where the picnic was. And they..."

She stopped there, started crying, her nose all clogged with tears and disgust. Her face buried in her hands and she kept crying. Noah himself had not seen such a deluge. I looked over at Dave. He was thinking the same thing as me.

"And then he ran off, left town, right after telling me." Her voice was choked with fear and sadness and a touch of anger. "He told me. He told me everything and said if I ever told anyone me and my kids would be next." She finally looked up with eyes red as hell and spewing the venom of a python. "He told me *everything.*"

She stood up and started pummeling me with her clubbed fists, as though I were him, Jeremy Collins, her husband, the evil that had lived with her and fathered her children. Dave started to take a step forward but I shook him off. I managed to grab her wrists and slow down her assault and look her in the eyes until she finally saw reality and the present. I slowly guided her back down, and her hands came together as though in prayer.

"Do you remember the girl's name?" I heard myself speaking to a suspect, interrogating them for answers or clues. I allowed myself to forget for a moment she was as much a victim in this as well.

"No."

Dave came alongside me trying to keep his voice low, knowing we were actively investigating a series of murders. From Mrs. Brayfield we had the name Kimberly. Figuring it was a father or brother we knew we would need her whole name.

"What do we do know, Baron?"

"I got someone at the *Traveler* who can help. And you better believe I'll be there first thing in the morning."

We started to leave and something in me returned to being human again.

"Mrs. Collins, I think Dr. Brenz will be able to release the body soon, if you were wanting to make funeral arrangements."

She looked up slowly, the eyes of a demon staring back at me.

"You can dump him in the river for all I give a damn."

I was thinking it didn't matter where on earth Jeremy Collins wound up. His final destination was Hell.

Chapter Eleven

Rain made me think of death. To Baron Witherspoon, the son of a farmer, it should have invoked thoughts of crops and harvest and the affirmation of Life. But to Eric Kimble, it brought back deep somber memories of mud and the foul stench of decay. At times I was a little Kimble covered up by a lot of Witherspoon. At times, I was neither, just an empty wandering shell, somehow aware of the truth and always denying it.

After trying to move quickly, I realized the rain was going to soak right through my clothes no matter what I did. I could have checked out a car but it was only five blocks to the *Traveler* building. Sandy Clevenger was waiting at the front door for me. She was short, barely five feet, with a shock of totally white hair and the kind of wrinkles reminding me of lines in an old tree that's been cut down. There was, however, a shine in her eyes as though there were miles and miles of roads inside her and tales to be told. Right now, I needed one of those tales.

We sat down at a large desk in a back room, wide catalogs with hard covers bound with metal brads laid out before us. These were the old editions, the ones recording the history of a town where the participants of the Cherokee Strip Land Run first came in anticipation and greed. At first, my heart sank figuring this was going to be like looking through the court files in the Cowley County Courthouse in Winfield. Sandy took off her glasses and looked at me like my old teacher would when checking on the progress of my homework assignment.

"What are you looking for?"

"A girl named Kimberly. Assaulted, maybe murdered. It was about twelve years ago."

Sandy's eyes lit up like a coin-operated pin game.

"I remember that," she blurted out and then started rummaging through the catalogs trying to find the exact one. "Sad, sad story."

"I didn't find anything in the files at the courthouse in Winfield."

"No one was brought to trial for it."

"Okay. But I didn't find anything either in the Ark City files. Surely a murder would have been investigated."

"One of the suspects had a brother on the force. Officer Robert Foster Collins." It all made sense now. Seems everyone knew about the late Jeremy Collins except no one had the decency to say anything.

She kept licking the tips of her main finger and going through page after page, trying to find the exact edition which held the story she unfortunately had remembered.

She stopped suddenly, slapped her hand down hard on the page, and turned it toward me to read. A young girl who was involved in the picnic assault at Parkerfield had been found brutally raped and murdered just out of town along the banks of the Arkansas River. A sharp knife had been used to cut her. Bruises were found all over her body. Her name was Kimberly.

Kimberly Dixon.

Sandy reached for my wrist, apparently worried I was going to tumble over from faint. The scars in my face, each line, pulsed as though I had been struck by lightning. I could feel my eyes blinking rapidly, something like tears filling up. It was the shell exploding in back of me all over again. This time there was no one there to save me.

All these years Natalie held something hateful and ugly within her. All these years, a monster was growing like the child she would never have. Carl Bottomley, Thomas Sutton, and Jeremy Collins had wiped out the last shred of human decency Natalie Dixon ever had and turned her into a vengeful spirit. On top of that, the police in the form of Jeremy Collins' brother had failed her.

I could have such a belief but only to myself. I could think she was innocent largely because I had fallen in love with her. My empathy allowed me to believe in her totally and completely. Then I felt a sick churning inside my stomach. I was a policeman and had to do what was right. Even when I had a chance to gun down Jake Hickey like a mad dog, I brought him in because I believed in justice and the law. It's not the way I grew up but it's what Baron Witherspoon would have wanted.

I walked out of the *Traveler* building, letting the rain come down and hoping it would wash me clean. I knew it never would. Maybe it would just wash me away.

It was important to find Natalie, to bring her in, to protect her, to help her. Beth was the first person I thought of. But as I ran toward her home, I couldn't figure out what to say, how to say it. My appearance alone would alarm her. Right then, finding Natalie was all that mattered.

It wasn't my intention to be knocking so hard on their front door. I was growing deaf from the torrents of rain, and I couldn't hear myself speak or walk. Beth opened the door; Frank was in the foyer just behind her.

"Sorry to bother you but I'm looking for your cousin." The polite tone of voice did not match the rain-soaked derelict on the front porch looking more like the town drunk asking politely for whiskey.

"Natalie?"

"Yes." My response was too quick, partially shouting over the rain which was falling harder. Frank stepped forward toward Beth, touched her elbow. She reached out an arm toward me.

"Baron, why don't you come in out of the rain?"

"I've got to find Natalie."

For the first time in her life, Beth looked at me as though I were a stranger. If she had any doubts about me after I had come back from the war, if she thought I was acting strange when a gangster was in our midst, she overlooked those differences. Now, I was a bedlamite, nothing as profound as St. John the Baptist, but a madman suffering delusions. It was the thought that triggered a memory of a conversation.

I didn't mean to laugh when Natalie mentioned the book of Amos in the Old Testament. I was thinking of the Amos and Andy show on the radio. I had never heard of it from the Bible. Apparently a minor prophet. She often quoted scripture even though she didn't profess to be religious. Out of the blue during one discussion she quoted Amos 5:24.

But let justice roll on like a river, righteousness like a never-failing stream.

We had gone fishing together. Jeremy Collins was found by the river. Natalie would meander along the banks of the Arkansas River. From the waters we had come and to the waters we would go.

I knew where to find her.

Chapter Twelve

There was something about the Arkansas River which could always draw Natalie like a prodigal child returning to the place she called home. It might have been the ebb and flow of time or the course life takes. I had discovered she was very learned on various topics but her comments seemed to be sifted through the clouds. Perhaps she was no longer connected to this earth, this time and place. Or maybe she hadn't been for a long time. It took a great deal of effort to maintain my own identity over the course of sixteen years. At first, I was ashamed of who I had been and uncertain how people might actually respond to Eric Kimble. After a while, I was neither Kimble nor Witherspoon even though I kept waking up each and every day. There was no telling why Natalie had given in to despair rather than reaching out for help. I couldn't judge knowing what I had been through. All I could do was try to save her, try to save the love I was sure we had.

I had no reason to believe she would be down by the river or anywhere else for that matter. Her mission had been fulfilled. The three men who raped and murdered her sister were dead: beaten, stabbed, and emasculated. The offending part had been removed. Yet I couldn't imagine where she would go, what kind of life she could go back to, or what her life had actually been all these years. The one favorite fishing spot was all that was left. It was a reminder of a simpler and quieter time for her.

The rain viciously pummeled the ground. Streets turned to mud like something out of an old Western town. Puddles gathered like miniature lakes, tadpoles in place of fish. I wore no hat or overcoat. I was no longer concerned about how wet I was because there was nothing I could do to stop it. My baptism was taking place. It might not have been enough to wash away all my sins.

The ground was treacherous but I continued to run in desperation, barely able to breathe, falling down twice, scraping my arm, letting blood and mud mingle, terrifying me with a reminder of a little piece of hell I once occupied. It was the war all over again. The wind picked up and my face grew numb from the cold. Droplets were constant on my eye lashes, making everything appear as if it were underwater.

The river had risen quite a bit, perhaps three feet or more. I saw her on the other side wearing a white dress, almost like it was a wedding gown. Unfortunately, as it was completely soaked, it no longer held its elegance. Her hair, which was typically constrained with bobby pins, was dangling and stringy, plastered to the side of her face. She walked, almost drifted along, seemingly carried by a cloud. However, one hand pressed firmly against her thigh, holding something, grasping it, not wanting to let it go.

"No one did anything about them," she said, her voice raised above the pounding of the rain. "They took her away from me. Used her and dumped her like garbage. She was such a beautiful little girl." She looked directly at me, her eyes fixed on mine. "What makes men do something so ghastly?"

I shook my head, not having any answers, only wanting to help ease her pain. The river rushed rapidly. I took a small step forward. She raised her hand from her side and I saw the knife. It was long, like a filet knife.

My heart skipped a beat. I felt something sharp stick in my throat. I wanted to speak but I couldn't. Even if I could, I didn't know what to say.

"They're gone now," she recited as though it were a Bible verse. "They're gone."

In one sudden, swift move, the filet knife was dragged firmly across her throat. Blood spurted and ran down her dress. The hand holding the knife dropped heavy and limp to her side and her fingers released the weapon. A faint ding echoed, like a distant church bell, as the knife hit the river rocks. Like a balloon that had been burst, Natalie crumpled, fell into the river, the splash echoing like a cannon, and she floated angrily away. A deep pain like a dagger pierced my chest. I shuddered, not from the cold, but from the empty feeling of loss. I dropped to my knees as though I were in prayer. I had never done that before. I knew I would never do it again.

I reported finding Natalie's body but left out any of the circumstances. Initially, Beth thought I figured her cousin might be in danger and the reason why I acted so crazed. However, it wasn't long before she just stopped speaking to me. Did she know all along? I couldn't tell. Female cousins are close and share many secrets, although I couldn't believe Beth would accept this knowledge without it bothering her in some way. The wall of gentility we had shared was shattered like a soap bubble. It was now the cruelty of the world standing like a brick building between us. She knew now the darkness of the world, of my world, and the knowledge changed everything.

Weeks passed with no further killings. I made it appear as though I were still researching, trying to formulate any new ideas, and present something to the chief. He made the executive decision to call the case inactive and advised me to continue on with other pending business. Our small town could not abide such killings and needed to move on to whatever future we were to have. Most of the cases were minor burglaries or drunk and disorderly calls. It didn't matter to me.

For a brief period of time, someone special had entered my life. Maybe I allowed her in or maybe she belonged there. The part of me that craved justice was in conflict with the law officer. What Natalie had done, if she had actually done it, was wrong and as foul and heinous as the crimes perpetrated against her beloved sister. The world, however, was not a lesser place with the loss of Bottomley, Sutton, and Collins. It might have even been safer.

It didn't matter what anyone else thought. Natalie's memory was secure with me. Her name would never be tarnished by the truth.

Part Two

The Brotherhood

Chapter Thirteen

Sometimes it can be difficult to gauge the passage of time. I suppose if you're a true farm boy you can tell. I wondered how long it had been since I had been in Chicago. Or France. Or how long since Natalie died. The first two seemed like a lifetime ago. The last, I realized, was only three years.

It is obvious cops can't keep a secret. After Mrs. McGuire passed away, her sister, Miss Banister, inherited ownership of the rooming house and continued to maintain it, largely because she didn't want to see anyone displaced. She also quietly mentioned she was glad to leave the big city (Wichita) and the demands of her single adult daughter. She soon became known to all as an inveterate baker, having offered some of her cakes and pies to Dixie at Daisy Mae's. However, when I saw Dave Morton suspiciously leave by a back door my brow furrowed.

When I got to the municipal building on Friday, the front lobby was quiet, empty, just the desk sergeant with his head buried in a pile of paper. He was usually alert, giving everyone who passed through the doors the once over. There was a silence like a morgue. The squad room doors were closed which was unusual. As I opened them, a loud and boisterous chorus of "Happy Birthday!" attacked me like a gust of wind on the plains. On the table was a very large cake, exquisitely decorated, another magnificent creation from Miss Banister, considering not a one of them could bake a cupcake.

I didn't think much about turning forty, except to acknowledge I was a twenty year veteran of the Great War. It might have seemed unnecessary to remind myself I was Baron Witherspoon and not Eric Kimble, and my birthday was today April 1, 1938 and not June 25 as I had remembered it. Even after all this time, I was of two minds, but now, at least, of one world. And consequently one birthday.

Chief Richardson came out from his office as the celebration became its noisiest. I thought at first he might come off as the school principal advising the boys they were out of line. Instead, a warm smile filled his face, a rarity for him. He shook my hand firmly, made a casual comment about my being a valued officer, took a sip of punch, and then retired back into his office. Unlike Chief Taylor who was forced to retire when they discovered a still on his property, Chief Richardson was a more by-the-book type of commander who focused on procedure and protocol. For him to show his human side was certainly appreciated.

Lee Jones had two pieces of cake on his plate. He shoveled it into his mouth so fast he could pass for a magician performing a disappearing act.

"You think that's fair?" I asked him of his double indulgence.

"I'm having Jay's piece."

"But he doesn't work here anymore."

"He'd have wanted me to have it." Lee smiled.

Jay Davis was so excited about the murder

investigation he figured nothing like it would ever happen again in Ark City. He applied for a position with the Wichita Police Department. Chief Richardson wrote him a strong recommendation. He was on his way to becoming Dick Tracy, at least in his own mind.

While there were plenty of grinning and smiling faces, mostly covered in frosting, a somber Dave Morton came over to me nonchalantly with a teletype printout in his hand. It made me fear the worst.

"Just got a report Martin Childers was killed in a car accident in Tulsa." As is typical, Dave was very matter-of-fact. We certainly didn't care much for the president of Kanotex, the largest oil refinery in the area, but we certainly didn't wish him any harm.

"Any details?"

"Single car. Nothing else indicated."

Something like this would not have warranted anything more than a passing comment at a later time. Dave squinted in thought.

"And?"

"Well, it seemed like Hallett got him pushed out at Kanotex."

"Was it Hallett or…?" Former Councilman Hallett had a lot of pull in his day, but we suspected the Mob was making a push into other states. Just as before, we couldn't prove anything. "Let's see who takes over the refinery and what their attitude is. That'll tell us something." I needed to break up the heavy mood. "Have a piece of cake."

I had to reconsider the fact former Councilman Hallett did not seek re-election and went back to maintaining his limited law practice. Several of the undesirables who worked at Kanotex were no longer to be seen anywhere in town. The old ways were slowly being swept aside. At this point it was yet to be seen what might replace it.

It was natural for me to think about Natalie Dixon and the possibility of a life with her. Strange as it seemed, in order to stop thinking about her, I looked into other examples of multiple killings by a single perpetrator. It was a way of trying to understand. Why did she bring herself to do it? Why did she keep it hidden and let it eat at her? Why couldn't someone see she was hurting and try to help? I might never figure it out but I had to try. I believe Sandy Clevenger's reading on other newspapers beside the *Traveler* gave her special insight into such crimes. Truth be told, as the secretary of the newspaper, she found other big city papers more fascinating. She gave me a list of things to look up in the library, going so far as to contact the head librarian, Mrs. Bentley, to let her know I was doing some research. We certainly didn't want Mrs. Bentley to be afraid of the local police.

The Whitechapel Killer in London, known as the Ripper and H.H. Holmes from Chicago were the most violent and deadly. But I knew of a Carl Panzram, originally from Minnesota, and a Peter Kurten from Germany, who were executed in 1930 and 1931, respectively. I knew about military plunderers and rich noblemen and women from long ago but all of it seemed distant, not connected to anything from today. Panzram and Kurten were vicious and without remorse, not on a mission of vengeance, but driven by some other demonic force. Panzram's career as a serial killer, rapist, arsonist, and burglar spanned nearly twenty-five years in nearly a dozen states. Kurten, on the other hand, had a nine-month killing spree in Dusseldorf. Time and geography didn't matter as both these men were pure monsters. Maybe I was justifying what Natalie had done. In trying to divert my thoughts from possibilities which no longer existed I wound up remorseful, just a dopey guy unable to connect to people in a social way.

The course of forty years had taken me from the tough streets of the North Side of Chicago to the madness of a global conflict to the supposedly quiet streets of a small Kansas town. I had been a thug, a soldier, a friend, a cop on a mission. Twenty years removed from the war and I still had dreams, not as bad as they used to be thanks to Dr. Brenz. Four years after 'Crazy' Jake Hickey's end and my childhood still lingered, not Baron Witherspoon's wholesome upbringing but Eric Kimble's rough-and-tumble youth. As it stood, I had been many things and nothing through forty years, and I still had the rest of my life.

Chapter Fourteen

I didn't like it when things were quiet. It wasn't based on a fear of something sneaky going on or perhaps unseen forces were planning a wave of devastation. Since I didn't have hobbies and was no longer actively seeking companionship of a personal nature, the peace and quiet led to profound boredom. You sit and take stock of your life and realize you are looking at the wide vista of an infinite corn field or a never ending dirt road, a great deal of emptiness with nothing filling it. I would go to the station, read reports, check the teletype, re-read reports, offer to help anyone and everyone, even empty trash cans for the janitor. Maybe Baron Witherspoon, the real guy, the Kansas farm boy who sought action and excitement and a sense of duty, maybe *he* wouldn't have minded. The new Baron Witherspoon, the boy who used to be Eric Kimble, was feeling his oats once again.

It reminded me too much of the war. Everyone could understand the loud clamor of battle, the uncertainty of sudden death, the bleak and gray surroundings. What most people had a hard time realizing were the times in between when the silence pierced your ears like a dull thud and your heart was beating so fast you thought it was going to pop right out of your chest. Those were the times you thought you were dead.

On occasion, my face felt as though it were a piece of paper sliding off my skull. There wasn't the pain of years past. Instead, it seemed as though the muscles were no longer able to hold on to the grafts quite as securely as they did. Perhaps this was due to the technique or my age. Dr. Brenz concurred with my suspicions and showed me some exercises and massages I could do. They looked funny when he did them in front of me so I did them only at home. Then, after looking in the mirror while doing them, I decided they seemed awkward to me as well.

I went and saw *The Adventures of Robin Hood* and laughed when it was appropriate and found myself churning in my seat during the sword fight scenes. I would love to have been Robin Hood, or at the very least, Errol Flynn. Having a devil-may-care attitude, being every guy's best friend, being every woman's dream, and fighting for what was right. Well, I figured I had the last one sewn up.

Miss Banister cooked and baked far more than Mrs. McGuire. This isn't a bad thing, except she kept offering me all sorts of things I wasn't quite used to eating. With the lack of activity and the extra cakes and cookies, my waistline was ballooning up.

I was daydreaming about Olivia De Havilland as Maid Marian when I was called into Chief Richardson's office. I eagerly stood at attention, waiting while he had his head bent over a folder and then ruffled through some papers on his desk. He hadn't yet looked up at me which was unusual.

"Wichita Police Department is requesting your presence for a...consultation." I didn't respond. I didn't understand what that meant. The chief finally looked up. "They've got a series of crimes similar to what you…worked on three years ago."

"The men who were brutally murdered?"

"Says here," he remarked holding up the folder, "several women have been stabbed. Among other things." Again, I remained silent. While our case was extreme, certainly for our part of Kansas, I was certain a big city like Wichita would have had the resources to investigate such a case.

"Why me, sir?"

"Seems they heard about your investigation and want your feedback." I nodded, as it was the only other thing I could think to do. "You can drive up today. Better pack a bag in case you have to stay a bit. Oh, and save your hotel and meal receipts and the department will reimburse you." At least now I had something to do.

As I started to walk out, I turned back and shut the door again.

"Chief, do they…know about me?"

"About what?"

"My, well, my face and, you know, my scars."

He dropped the folder on his desk, flustered but trying to hide it with a moderate anger.

"Witherspoon, you're a police officer. They're police officers. They are currently investigating what appear to be horrific killings. They are not going to be concerned with your war wounds."

I nodded and politely left his office knowing there were many people who would not consider these merely war wounds but something closer to a monster like Frankenstein. They were so keen on having me assist them; what would they think when they saw me?

My doubts did not go away.

As I went home to pack a small satchel, I became more annoyed at Chief Richardson's cavalier attitude. Being a cop didn't mean you were part of some brotherhood. Maybe in a bigger city like Wichita. But I knew all kinds of guys who were policemen in Ark City and they were just, well, guys. Farm boys. Transplants from other areas. Just guys looking for a job. Moreover, they were human with the same fears and prejudices as anyone else. Baron Witherspoon or not, when I came back from Europe with a face resembling a scarecrow, it took a while for people to look at me, I mean really look into my eyes. These were people who had known Baron Witherspoon all their lives and even they found it difficult to have any kind of face to face conversation.

I had to believe in the chief, had to accept his notions. Going up there to help out was part of my duty and obligation. I took no issue with that. If I were to have a negative attitude about it beforehand, I would be incapable of offering assistance in the way they needed it. Beside my bag, I brought a notebook I had started, almost like a journal of all my readings in these types of crimes. You never think it could happen again but it is always best to be prepared.

Parked in the department's garage was a rickety Model A Ford, 4-cylinder no one was using at the time. The bumpiness of the ride and the incessant squeaks as it bounced were probably the reason. In order to drown out the noise on my nearly hour and a half drive, I thought of Natalie. At first, she was the subject of a murder investigation. I guess my mind thought this way on account of the reason for my journey. But I couldn't think of her as a criminal or how she ended up. I never knew her when she was younger, never saw the lovely young lady and sweet older sister she had been. Several times the word 'maybe' popped in my head, followed by 'what if.' I knew the past couldn't be changed. I just went back to listening to the squeaks and feeling the bumps in the road.

Ahead of me was another challenge. It was what I had to focus on. That and whatever future I was to really have.

Chapter Fifteen

I remember reading a book about Richard the Lionheart, journeying from England to the Holy Land on the Crusades, seeking to kick out the infidels, praise the Lord, and ransack the magnificence of Jerusalem. It was my own interpretation. I can only imagine what it must have been like for him to emerge from the desert and gaze upon the splendor before him.

Wichita was nothing like a holy city, although it surpassed anything I had seen since growing up in Chicago and a darn sight more fast-paced than Ark City. There were by far more cars which meant more frustrated drivers. If more women fancied being behind a steering wheel, it might have been catastrophic.

By the time I arrived in the city, all thoughts preoccupying my mind seemed to vanish like an afternoon spring rain. I was on an assignment and nothing else occurred to me. It took a bit to find the police headquarters. I didn't realize they made them as big as it was. Seemed more like a castle to me.

I walked in through the front entrance, head held high, a feeling of pride because I was being asked to assist in something so important. When Jay Davis ran up to me, I understood where the whole thing started. I wasn't too cocky to believe I had earned a large reputation from my showdown with Jake Hickey or my investigations into horrific murders. Somehow, Jay

Davis blabbed to his fellow cops in Wichita about a hotshot cop named Baron Witherspoon in his old town of Ark City who was real smart and could probably help out. I was hoping he didn't build me up too much.

"You made it," he said, a smile plastered across his face.

"So it was you?"

He leaned in close, like we were speaking of the Devil while in church.

"It's been real bad. No one wants to admit it. I figured you had more know-how than most of what they got passing off as detectives."

He wrapped his arm around my shoulder and started guiding me through the station house. I noticed other officers turning away, not even saying anything to Jay. My earlier bravado was starting to dwindle. It's not that I had any doubts about myself or concerns about my appearance. The whole notion of not knowing who I was when looking into a mirror, the conflict between being Eric Kimble and becoming Baron Witherspoon, the uncertainty about the future—all of this had been brought under control to a point where I could manage living each and every day. It wouldn't have bothered me if a young child stared at me or cried or even laughed. But these were police officers, like me, who, one would imagine, had seen far worse things than a man with a scarred face. Without so much as speaking with me, it hurt knowing I was already being rejected.

The painted name on the glass door was CHIEF O.W. WILSON. Jay stopped suddenly.

"I told them you were what we needed. Don't disappoint me." He smiled like a kid handing in his term paper and hoping he wouldn't flunk.

A brief rap on the door was followed by a gruff response to enter. Chief Wilson sat behind the largest office desk I had ever seen, head down looking through a thick file of paper and photos. Behind him were a U.S. flag and the flag of the state of Kansas, placed like columns surrounding him. Citations of all kinds were on the wall. A photo of the chief with former governor Alf Landon and another photo of him with President Roosevelt hung like proud children just behind him between the two flags, each photo closest to the flag which represented them correctly. A theater stage could not have been set up more appropriately.

When Chief Wilson finally looked up, he stared at me. His face was blank, without any emotion, not giving away his thoughts. I'm sure he was trying to reconcile the description of me given to him by Officer Jay Davis and the strange looking man before him.

"You Witherspoon?" he asked. There was a tone of uncertainty in his voice.

"Yes, sir," I replied at full attention, harkening back to the army days. As far as I was concerned, Chief Wilson was my superior officer.

"We've been plagued with a series of murders our detectives have thus far been unable to crack. Officer Davis here says you have a certain degree of experience in these matters."

Realizing this wasn't a military base and Chief Wilson didn't require the spit-and-polish attitude, I let my shoulders fall and allowed my tone to be more conversational.

"As Chief Richardson may have indicated, I was the lead officer investigating three rather brutal murders no one in our jurisdiction had ever previously encountered."

"And Chief Richardson indicated the case was never solved." It wasn't a question. He already knew the answer. It finally dawned on me Chief Wilson never wanted an outside party coming in to his investigation. Perhaps he had politicians like we had in Ark City who, shall we say, insisted he do everything possible to find a solution to his problems. Jay would take a lot of heat if I didn't come through. Chief Wilson was not going to be supportive thinking someone other than his own men might solve the case even if it meant further murders. He was also not going to act like he was the host of a cocktail party, either.

"We believe we had a viable suspect who more than likely died as there were no further killings. We also feel our investigation was close to apprehending the suspect based on all our research and discovery. In essence, the case was solved, sir. We just didn't have the necessity of a trial." It was like slowly pushing a blade into his gut. I knew where he stood; it was time for him to get to know a little bit about my attitude.

His tight-lipped stare reminded me of an ancient oak tree, firmly embedded with roots as deep as the earth's core. This man was the type who was always right. I had to maintain my dignity and honor as a police officer regardless of the local politics at work.

"Davis, go get Roach. He'll be Officer Witherspoon's...liaison." He threw the word away like used butcher's paper.

Jay made no effort to make eye contact as he left. He understood the situation as clearly as I did. I stood there before Chief Wilson in his office for what seemed like the length of a Catholic funeral mass. Despite nothing being said, there were strange sounds, ceiling fan moving papers, the tapping of his fingernail on the file, the sounds a room makes despite the fact it is not a living thing.

The office door opened suddenly.

The cleaned, pressed and starched uniform and the meticulously combed hair were the only things indicating this individual was a police officer. He was somewhere in the neighborhood of five foot six inches and had the angelic face of a teenager in his high school years. His eyes had the kind of clarity found in a country stream on a warm summer day. He looked more like an usher at a wedding than a member of law enforcement in the largest city on Kansas.

"Roach, you're familiar with Officer Witherspoon from Arkansas City?"

"Yes, sir. Officer Davis had apprised me of Officer Witherspoon's arrival."

"Show him every courtesy, including access to all files and the detectives working on the case." Chief Wilson's tone was matter-of-fact and not inviting. I was a party crasher but I was here and not going anywhere.

The young officer turned sharply like a soldier, opened the door for me, and we stepped out.

"It's Roché," he said softly. "Ronald Roché. These guys don't know how to pronounce it properly."

"Like 'Le Grenouille', Guy Roché, the Canadian bootlegger?"

He smiled for the first time.

"Same name, yes. But my mother would absolutely die if he were related to us."

I took further notice of his uniform and manners.

"I haven't seen this kind of discipline since my

army days," I casually commented.

"If I am to be taken seriously, Officer Witherspoon, I need to present myself professionally and never back down."

Our footsteps echoed down a long hallway. With his shoulders firm and his back straight, I imagined Officer Roché had far more to him than his fellow officers realized.

Chapter Sixteen

The large room where I was escorted contained four desks, all with phones, lamps, and several files on them. Roché advised me this was the special office occupied by the top detectives in the department, two of who were working on this case. Currently, the room was empty.

"Hmm, they said they would be here to meet you."

"Who?"

"Rackler and Sells. They're the two assigned to the case."

Like a vaudeville show, two large men entered on cue. The first one was younger, maybe in his mid thirties, built like a war horse but with a look of total anger and chaos, eyes that seemed to stare rather than see. There was something bullish about him, as though he were a runaway train, rolling over anybody and anything in its path. The man behind him was a good ten to fifteen years older than me, as big but seeming more like a large sack of flour with the same pale whiteness, looking like he had just awoken from a sound sleep. His steps fell heavy as he walked.

"This the guy?" blurted the younger man.

Roché pointed to the first and then the second man.

"Detective Rackler and Detective Sells, this is Officer Witherspoon from the Arkansas City…"

"I know who he is." Rackler's words cut like a

bayonet through a soft body, making my outstretched hand seem useless. "I told the chief we don't need him."

"John, back off." Sells' voice was like the bark of a stray dog. He reached out and shook my hand. "Charlie Sells. This guy is John Rackler. Just made detective last year and has something to prove." I squeezed a small smile and prevented it from showing on my face.

"I've already proven it." The stare was directed at me. He held it there, not flinching from the scars on my face. "Heard you were in the war." I didn't hear a tone of respect included in the comment. It wasn't even much of a question. Truth be told, he didn't seem to care.

Sells guided us over to their desks where there was only a spare chair. Officer Roché stood to the side, knowing he didn't quite fit into this circle.

"We've all been under a little bit of a strain here. Haven't had killings like these since I've been a cop so naturally it's got us rattled." He spoke like a father announcing to his family they had lost the farm.

"We're not rattled. We've got this thing…"

"John, shut up!" I was liking Sells more and more. A veteran of a police department, like myself, who had been through far more than any of the younger guys who felt a need to show they belonged. We both knew all you had to do was be there, show up, stay the course, and you'd find your way. Running like a mad dog through a crowded marketplace was going to do more damage than good.

"My partner thinks he knows everything there is to know about murder investigations," Sells said softly. "Kind of funny seeing how this is his first one."

"But not yours." I didn't have to ask because I knew this kind of cop. It was more of an acknowledgement.

"First one was '08. Just got on the force. Landlady said she had heard an argument between a couple one night, then it was quiet the whole next day. She unlocked the apartment door. I found the wife. Throat slit. Blood everywhere."

I shivered which I guess they took for being scared or soft. I was just thinking back to Heather Devore and Natalie Dixon. I couldn't understand why men got shot and stabbed but ladies had their throat slit.

"I wasn't the detective on that one. But it was the first dead body I'd ever seen."

"And now?"

He pushed a large file in front of me, at least three inches thick. There were photos of bodies and the locations where they were found; reports from the medical examiner at least two to three pages per victim; witness statements; and a map of the city with markings indicating where the crimes occurred. It was overwhelming, not because of the crimes themselves but because of the extent of the documentation. When I was investigating our three killings in Ark City, there was myself and Dave Morton and a clerk from the Cowley County Courthouse, plus Dr. Brenz in his unofficial capacity as a de facto medical examiner and Sandy Clevenger with the newspaper clippings from the *Traveler*. Perhaps, at the moment, I was feeling dismissive of this big city department, thinking they should have been able to figure this out by now with everything they had before them. It was then I realized with a mindset like Detective Rackler they would never solve this because they couldn't think like the killer.

"John, why don't you go get the medical examiner's report from the latest victim?"

"Why can't Roach here get it?"

"Why don't you both go?" Officer Roché understood the subtlety of Detective Sells' request by the small smirk apparently only I noticed. Rackler simply huffed and turned sharply.

"So, what's the story with the scars?"

I went into detail about my injury in the war and how it changed me, at first by sending me into a deep blue mood and then making me realize I still had a place in the world. I talked about all the things "Officer Witherspoon" had gone through and briefly touched upon the Jake Hickey encounter.

"One mean son of a bitch, wasn't he?"

"His type is gone now. Long gone." I was sounding more hopeful than I felt.

"Yeah, but what's in its place?" He raised an eyebrow, nodded, understood how one bad thing often easily replaces another.

It was time to bring the conversation back around to the reason I was sent to Wichita. "Have you had any suspects at all?"

"Interviewed a couple of guys." He pulled a notebook out from his inside jacket pocket and flipped it to one of the first pages. "There was Shane Norman, a dishonorably discharged army soldier. He was arrested for breaking up a bar while drunk. Background check indicated reason for discharge was assault on women where he was stationed in Georgia. Had an alibi for the first and third murders." Sells flipped more pages. "Oh yeah, this guy. Mexican named Rene Cristales. One mean son of a gun. Domestic disturbance with his common law wife. We found a bunch of knives and machetes at his house in a storage shed. No alibi until the so-called wife recanted her story and gave him one. I had Rackler follow him a couple of days but nothing came up. Just not finding anyone crazy enough to pin this on."

We discussed the similar crimes in Ark City from three years prior. He then told me how I got involved. A casual comment he made in a meeting with Chief Wilson and City Manager Bert Wells found its way to the mayor who was bothered by the lack of an arrest or viable leads. He was fuzzy on how Jay Davis made mention of me but the next thing he knew he and Rackler were in the chief's office where everyone was yelling. Rackler was taking offense, seeing this as a slur either on his detecting skills or his manhood. The chief felt this was making the department look bad and would jeopardize his job. And Sells just wanted the case closed no matter what it took.

"So, you went to bat for me?"

His brow wrinkled in deep thought. This was followed by what appeared to be a maniacal smile on his face as though an insane clown had taken his place.

"No. I didn't want you here either. I've been in the Wichita Police Department for thirty years. Figured on retiring soon. That's what the wife wants. I sure as heck do not want to go out with this case left open. And I certainly don't want some farm boy cop from the sticks telling me how to close it. But you're here now and I will extend a professional courtesy to you. I'll keep Rackler off your back and work with you. You find anything, you figure anything out, you better come to me with it. You understand?"

It was almost as though I was looking down from above and seeing myself as a knight or rook or pawn on a chess board. I realized it was no different than what I had previously experienced. The politicians ran things and moved all of us around as little pieces for their amusement. I couldn't really blame Sells or Rackler. Cops didn't like feeling pushed around. By the same token, I definitely didn't like it coming from a fellow cop.

"Detective Sells, there is nothing I would like better than to be back home in my nice little farm boy town, arresting drunks on a Friday night pay day or grabbing a kid trying to steal a car. But I'm here and I'm not running back to Ark City because a bunch of big city boys don't feel like asking for help when they need it."

We looked at each like two gunslingers in the middle of Dodge City. Maybe one of us was Wyatt Earp. Maybe neither one of us was. We knew we were going to tolerate each other as much as we had to and then no more. Unfortunately, we didn't know how long it might be.

Chapter Seventeen

I walked out of the office slowly, carefully, trying not to let anyone see I had the shakes. It felt like everything was falling apart and I wasn't referring just to a case. I went to Arkansas City, Kansas after the war because I could hide out, become Baron Witherspoon, and figure out where to go from there. As the years passed, I was like a cottonwood tree firmly rooted in the soil and growing tall and straight. It didn't matter what you called me because people knew who I was, at least in their own minds.

To be questioned and doubted stripped me of whatever armor I had been wearing for all these years. Maybe I wasn't so smart or so important or so respected. Certainly not feared. Fortunately, Officer Roché was standing in wait for me, allowing me to regain some of my composure.

"I'm very sorry about that, Officer Witherspoon. To come all this way to be treated so poorly is…"

"Don't worry. I've dealt with tougher birds." The most important thing I should have done was to go through the file meticulously but I needed to get out of the building, needed to breathe something other than the stale air of neglect. "The file indicated the first murder was a girl who worked in a laundry but the second was a pro skirt." He looked at me with eyes as blank as a newborn baby. "A prostitute."

"Yes. Sorry. I didn't quite catch…"

"The prostitute, did she work alone or did she have a pimp?"

His slightly casual demeanor disappeared in favor of a stiff and stone-cold mouthpiece. I didn't think I had offended him but I could tell from the tone of his voice this subject made him feel uncomfortable.

"She seemed to be in the employ of a man named Carson Stankey."

"Where do we find this guy?"

Ronald Roché turned like a soldier and marched out. I followed not knowing where we were headed. I was grateful to be in the company of someone who seemed so knowledgeable about the facts of the case despite not being directly involved. Already he had proven more useful than a mere liaison. I wondered how he might hold up against the rougher elements in this city.

The Delano district was established back in the days of cattle drives. It was an area of gambling and prostitution frequented by cowboys who were not looking for respectable diversion. The establishment we went to was neither a bar nor a restaurant. It had five or six tables around which there were two or three chairs apiece. A curtain covered the entrance to a back room. A short man with a thick moustache and thicker arms and shoulders stood nonchalantly by the curtain. His eyes moved from left to right and back again. There were two men at one table with highballs. I couldn't tell what they were drinking. The only light came from the glass panel on the front door.

After walking in, Officer Roché simply stopped. I didn't want to approach the man at the curtain and leave the kid standing at the door. I took two steps forward and looked directly at Mr. Moustache.

"We're looking for Carson Stankey."

"This is a private club."

Like an emcee or magician, a tall bald man appeared from behind the curtain. He had a shiny black goatee trimmed into a neat point and deep amber eyes. They glistened in the minimal sunlight. His face was smooth like a whitewashed fence and as pale. A cigarette hung loosely from his lips, most of the ash still connected to what remained. He had the vague appearance of some fallen European aristocrat who still maintained a regal aura.

"It's all right, Montisse. We can make an exception for the police." His lips barely moved. The ash remained. I stared straight at him. I wanted him to see my face, get a good look at it, and perhaps wonder as much about me as I was about him. "More questions regarding Chantelle?"

Ronald came closer to me, speaking softly though not whispering as it might have appeared rude.

"The second victim."

The bald man scowled, finally taking notice of me.

"You wear a uniform but look like no cop I've ever seen." He stepped forward with a feline gracefulness. "Carson Stankey, at your service."

I accepted his extended hand. The grip was firm, capable of squeezing the life from a man's neck or pulling firmly on the trigger of a gun. My guess was Carson Stankey fancied himself more of an intellectual business man and less of a gutter pimp. The establishment we were in told a different story.

"Officer Baron Witherspoon from Arkansas City.

I'm here consulting with the Wichita Police Department on the series of murders of, well, ladies of shady means."

A smile emerged like a child from behind its mother's apron.

"Ark City police. Consulting with our own esteemed department. Very interesting." He paused, the smile held as tightly as a child holding a balloon. "Why?" It was then the smile disappeared completely.

"I have certain, shall we say, knowledge in this field."

We continued staring at each other. I wasn't aware of Roché's presence or of Montisse. I had lost my point of reference getting caught up in game of cat-and-mouse with a tiger.

"And how may I be of assistance?"

"Was there anyone who would have wanted to hurt Chantelle?"

"She worked in a rough business with rough men."

"You don't seem all broken up about her death."

"There are many girls. What is the loss of one?"

"Perhaps she was a problem. Perhaps she had information about, oh, other business activities. Perhaps…"

"*Perhaps* is a small word used by small men."

It was my turn to smile. I had allowed him to speak and I had figured him out. And I was going to tell him what he needed to know.

"Hiding behind a curtain will not save you. You figure her death was a warning to you. But there were others after. Not your girls but similar. Maybe someone is threatening your business. Or you. You're not so smart, Stankey. You think puffing out your chest can scare off the police. Well, with all these killings, there's going to be more police around. Sure, they're looking for a killer. But while they're at it, they'll flip you up one side and down the other. Either way this private club of yours is going to get public real soon."

It was a mistake to turn my back, not on him but on Montisse who I hadn't yet sussed out. I was hoping Officer Roché would cover me if needed. We walked out safely, back into the light.

"I've never known of anyone to talk to him so directly," Ronald said in amazement, practically breathless. I had earned myself a new admirer.

What he didn't realize was everything I said was a bluff. No one was killing prostitutes just to undermine a business. Not even the Chicago gangs took out working girls for the sake of business. From trying to figure out the mind of a killer three years ago, I started picking up signs. Some made sense; old notions were thrown out. However, with the attitude of most of the Wichita Police Department, I didn't know how long of a chance I'd get.

Chapter Eighteen

I had dealt with the oily charm of Councilman Hallett and the back-slapping back-stabbing nature of Martin Childers. Never had I come across a man so cold and distant from anything human as this Carson Stankey. Not even Jake Hickey. Yet, I could see beneath the tough veneer he was afraid of something. I just didn't know him well enough to know what it was.

There were more people to visit. As I had only briefly glanced at the file, there was no recollection of the next victims.

"Were any more of his girls killed?" I asked Roché.

"No. The next two were girls named Angela and Aurora. They worked for Miss Becky."

"And who is Miss Becky?"

"She runs a house between here and Riverside. Old house. Many rooms."

"You ever been there, Ron?" I wasn't trying to embarrass him or put him on the spot but he talked about the place with a quaint familiarity. He acted as though a metal rod had been slid up inside his shirt causing him to stand more erect than the thought of those girls.

"No, sir." His eyes looked away as he answered, almost ashamed at the notion.

We started to move on then I stopped and grabbed

his arm.

"You sure know a lot about this case."

"I've been following it, sir. I hope to make detective some day."

He started to remind me of Jay Davis, just a young kid, uneducated in life and the world in all its glory and its stains, hoping to make a mark, hoping to move up and out of whatever had trapped him and held him back. I could tell he was thought of as a mosquito by his fellow officers. Maybe his height or his boyish face didn't set too well with men who were trying to be tough and maintain their sense of strength. Rackler was one of those guys. Maybe they had an opening and just promoted him to get him off the streets as a beat cop. He was the kind of guy who could explode in a rage at the drop of a hat, one you did not want to cross especially if Sells was nowhere in sight. I wondered if Ronald Roché had the wherewithal to stand up to someone like Rackler. Then again, the mongoose is capable of taking down the snake.

The house on Athenian just south of McLean Boulevard was far more regal than anything I had ever seen in Ark City with architecture reserved for wealthier denizens. As I was a city boy, all I ever remembered were tall brick and concrete buildings with suites and apartments resonating with class and money. This house, from the outside, exuded with opulence and more. Steep roof, arched windows, a couple with stained glass, a full covered porch wrapping all the way around at least as I could see, painted a deep green with a light tan trim. She was a proud lady demanding attention and respect. It was a rather odd sensation for a house where gentlemen would go to take their pleasure.

Ronald rang the doorbell and a young colored girl answered. At first, I took her to be some kind of servant until the door opened more and she was dressed in an elegant satin dress.

"We're here to see Missy Becky."

The young girl smiled cordially, opened the door wider, and directed us by her extended arm to a parlor. The arm was smooth, a glistening softness in a pale coffee color, contrasted against large green eyes like those of a cobra. She was a vision of some man's dream but could also be a dangerous trap.

There were two armless chairs of carved wood with plush seat and back cushions and a small sofa made of the same wood with matching cushions. Two end tables each contained a small crystal decanter with a purplish liquid and two small glasses for each. The fireplace had not been lit since the previous winter. There were various pieces strewn about: porcelain, glass, ivory. It was like a small museum. Yet there was nothing personal in the room. No photos or books, nothing to identify this as a home where people lived and were considered as human.

The woman who glided down the steps was in her late forties, clear skin without wrinkles but with a certain weariness. She wore a flowing gown and her shoulders were covered with a lace shawl. She was attractive enough to be one of her own employees. She held out her hand waiting for attention. I accommodated her.

"I assume you gentleman are here on your business and not for mine."

"Officer Baron Witherspoon of the Arkansas City Police Department."

With the wave of her arm, she invited us to sit in the chairs while she sat on the sofa. It was the same gesture as the young colored girl. They all had been trained in the propriety of charm.

"Sherry?" she offered.

"No thank you, ma'am." She poured herself a glass. I don't think he realized it but Ronald tugged at his collar as if in a noose.

"Something wrong, officer?" she asked him. There was a whimsical coyness in her tone.

"Officer Roché is not used to such establishments."

"And you are?"

"I was in the war."

She lifted her glass in a toast to my assumed heroism.

"Have you discovered who murdered my girls?"

"Not yet. We are working very hard on this case. Can you tell me something about the girls? Did they live here?"

"They could have. They chose not to." There was the bitter disappointment of a parent emerging. She looked away for a moment, perhaps blaming herself. "I understood completely. Young ladies need a sense of independence."

"What can you tell me about the night each of them was killed?"

"Aurora left very late. She was, well, entertaining a couple of visiting college football players. They had played against Wichita University, lost, and became so inconsolable they sought out the comforts to be found in this house." I smiled realizing there were many ways to describe the acts between a man and a woman, some of which didn't admit to illegal acts. "One young man waited on the other who was with Aurora. They were busy for a good long time."

"Inconsolable as you say," I reminded her.

"They left shortly before midnight and Aurora shortly thereafter."

"The young men. Were they angry or upset?"

"No, Officer Witherspoon. On the contrary. They felt much better upon their departure. Regrettably, Aurora was killed that night."

"And Angela?"

"She told me she was feeling poorly. I believe it was a womanly thing. She left before the evening began. It was still daylight."

"Did she have any visitors who were belligerent or acting mean toward her?"

"Angela was one of the sweetest young girls I had ever known. Always a smile on her face. Never an unkind word."

I stood up and Ronald followed my cue. I reached for her hand to kiss it again.

"Thank you for your time. We'll see our way out."

Ronald walked ahead of me quickly, almost tripping over his feet.

"Officer Witherspoon?"

I turned gallantly. Something about the house and Miss Becky made me feel like a knight of the Round Table.

"Yes, ma'am."

"Why are you up here all the way from Arkansas City?"

"I have experience in these matters."

For the first time, she looked closely at me, saw my scars, looked into my eyes, probably remembering my comment about the war. We both dealt in matters of the flesh but from different perspectives. I knew of hers; she did not know of mine.

Chapter Nineteen

Standing with my hands on my hips, I gazed at the big beautiful house, trying to imagine what kind of man would look upon it and its residents as something to defile in such a vicious way. While it might not have been a place I would have frequented, the evil perpetrated upon the women made no sense. It suddenly dawned on me I had assumed a man was responsible for the killings in Ark City so now I would have to start my thought process all over again. If I kept making assumptions it could result in more deaths.

I instructed Ronald to bring me back to the station house so I could review the files completely. I knew I wouldn't be able to take them home as I did in my own town. He took me to an empty office just down from the detectives' room figuring I wouldn't want to spar with those boys all over again. He retrieved the file and brought it to me. There was a desk with a lamp and some file cabinets. It was an interior office with no windows and had the smell of disuse and abandonment. It was perfect for someone who wasn't supposed to be there in the first place.

"Did you learn anything from Carson Stankey or Miss Becky?" he asked, his head cocked like a puppy dog.

"They didn't seem to care, probably afraid of getting in trouble. But they're both scared."

"Of what?"

"A monster."

Just as I had done three years ago, I reviewed every piece of evidence. I looked at every photo of the women who were killed, all stabbed in various parts of their torso, almost all near their abdomen and below. I read every medical report. There was a map of the city with markings indicating the locations. The only thing striking was the first woman was not a prostitute of any kind but a young girl who worked in a laundry. She was pretty like the rest with long blonde hair, a slight shade of red in it. Soft thin lips and freckles on a pale face indicated this girl was barely twenty. She looked nothing like the made-up young women who had far more world weariness. There was nothing to connect her to the others. I also didn't see the hatred like I did in Natalie's victims. A smash to the skull. Multiple stabbings to incapacitate. A final slice to show disrespect. The medical examiner's reports indicated "one or two slow incisions with some upward movement or twisting within the thoracic cavity." From what I could gather in the photos and drawings, the killer stood facing his victim, stabbed them in the stomach area likely unexpectedly, and either drew the knife up toward the heart or twisted it within the confines of the point of entry. This indicated precision and a controlled process. If there was anger, it was being suppressed. Carson Stankey was a brute who played the part of a gentleman. If aroused, he would act more like a wild stallion that hadn't been broke. Miss Becky, to my mind, was the kind of lady who would use poison so she could watch a girl die slowly and painfully before her. The only thing I guessed was this killer had somehow enjoyed these kills as they give him (or her) an undefined pleasure. If I could figure out what that pleasure was, I might have a better idea of who was behind all of this.

The frustrating thing was I was alone on this. While I had the obedient police liaison, the detectives actually working the case, the police chief, and more than likely everyone all the way up to the mayor were not going to lift a finger to help the disfigured intruder I represented.

Unbeknownst to me, it was getting late. A room without a window is not the ideal way for an obsessed man to tell time. Fortunately, Officer Roché knocked politely on the door and entered quietly.

"Got it all solved?" His smile was big, warm, and friendly. It was the first time today he didn't appear scared of his own shadow.

"Not quite." I was tired, the tone of my voice rather dull. I didn't mean to take away his good mood but my mind was spinning in all directions.

"The chief got you a room at the Carey House. I can take you there."

"I've got my own car."

"Oh, yeah. Sure. I forgot."

I stood up and stretched, realizing I had been sitting in one position for the better part of three hours. I pushed the file across the desk toward him and started to walk out.

"I'll need you tomorrow."

"Great. Yes, I'll make myself available."

He gave me brief directions, indicating it was on the corner of Douglas and St. Francis, certain I wouldn't miss it. As he walked me out, he told me the story of how Carrie Nation came in with her hatchet and chopped at the bar and threw a big rock at the mirror on the wall, smashing it loudly. All this in the name of temperance.

"Well," I commented, "everyone seems to have something they're against."

"What are you against, Officer Witherspoon?"

"Murder."

He was right about it being easy to find. The clerk reminded me of Phil Garmes but only swarthy like an imitation Valentino. The pencil thin moustache looked more like a caterpillar on his lip and there was enough grease in his hair to light an oil lamp. He did, however, find my reservation quickly, handed me my key, and allowed me to walk off mumbling my thanks without spitting at me.

The room was spacious but my eyes found only the bed. I sat down enjoying its comfort then reached down in my bag for a bottle of hooch I brought along. Sometimes I still had headaches and sometimes I still had dreams. I figured this case was going to bring them both back and they did.

I started to realize I had the ability to read these reports and figure out the person behind it, almost as though I were looking through their eyes. Any other policeman's stomach would be churning. It was times like these I doubted my own sanity. All the years working with Dr. Brenz and coming to terms with who I was, had been born, and who I had become. Most days I was actually proud of myself.

I guess Natalie rattled me a bit, perhaps because I thought I could possibly settle down with her. When the opportunity passed, I was lost again, figuring I would be a cop until I wasn't anymore, and watching my face sag and the scars become sad bitter reminders of a painful transformation.

Before I knew it, half the bottle was gone.

Chapter Twenty

The morning felt like a dream. Waking up in a different bed in a strange room, the light shining through lace curtains and reflecting off polished bed posts all made me feel as though I had died and gone to some kind of heaven but not anything I was aware of or expected. It was almost exactly the same thing in the hospital in France, face wrapped like an Egyptian mummy, little slits left for my eyes to try to focus on my surroundings, arms tied down to the bed to prevent me from tearing off the bandages. On this morning, my arms simply flailed as I saw Jake Hickey walking toward me and turn into Natalie Dixon right before she became Baron Witherspoon who whispered "Eric, it's your turn now."

My head wasn't pounding but it was spinning. Drawing back the lace curtains revealed an early Wichita, Kansas morning on Douglas Ave. It was my turn now.

The diner I stopped in for breakfast was nothing like Daisy Mae's. There was no one like Dixie behind the counter, and the looks I got made it feel like Halloween. I gobbled a helping of biscuits and gravy, washing it down with dark mud-thick black coffee and left. I was yearning for home.

I went to the detective's room to meet with Officer Roché. Detective Rackler was walking toward his desk, a cup of coffee in one hand and a thick file in the other.

"So, you solve the case yet?"

It would have been easy to respond, almost too easy. Rackler was a bully, probably since grade school. He liked nothing more than to be on top in an argument, whether or not he was right. It was probably because he had hardly ever been right. He pushed and if you pushed back he won the fight before you even started. Detective Sells came into the room shortly after Rackler's comment, his glance darting between us. He walked over to me calmly with an expectant look on his face. He didn't have to ask anything but still expected an answer.

"I interviewed Carson Stankey and Miss Becky," I said. "I don't think they know anything."

"That's what I figured." I wasn't sure if he was validating my efforts or indicating his lack of faith in my abilities. "Now what?"

"Two more murders. Two more interviews."

"You think you're going to find something we didn't?"

"Detective Sells, this is not a race or a game. I'm just doing what I was asked to do."

"I didn't ask you."

He turned sharply and walked to his desk. Fortunately, my liaison came in and provided me with the excuse to leave.

"From now on," I told Roché, "we meet in the other office. They don't want my help, and I don't need them getting in my way."

"Yes, sir," he replied with a smile. It was as though I were his big, older brother who was there to protect him. The truth was I cared less about another city's horrific murders than I did my own reputation. I figured some politicians were turning up the heat. I had experienced it before. But why a seasoned vet like Sells would give in was beyond me. A couple of interviews, a thoughtful consideration, a detailed report was about all they were going to get from me.

Melinda Malone ran a theater group that was performing at the Holland Theater just down the street from the hotel where I was staying. Song and dance and comedic sketches filled the bill. The troupe was largely made up of newer performers, those looking to make it in the legitimate theater if only someone of importance were watching in the audience. The shock of the killing of one of her performers was not enough for her to cancel any shows. Malone had a sweet face, smooth skin, and clear blue eyes but those tightly pursed lips indicated she had the bite of a lioness. She was maybe a couple of years younger than me but she responded with a yawn of boredom and weariness.

The dancer with dreams of being a ballerina was a Russian émigré named Valeria Delsin. She was quiet, reserved, most likely a virgin, according to Malone. Delsin preferred a walk in the night air after a show, perhaps reminding her of the coolness of a Moscow evening. It was a quaint story, one I knew didn't hold water. Show biz folks think everyone will fall for a line.

"They found her in an alley in back of the theater. Can you imagine that? She was nowhere to be found for the show the next night. I get all upset with her. And then, poof, they find her out back. Made me feel a bit uneasy. You know?"

I smiled because I had no response to her lack of compassion.

"Do you mind if I talk to the rest of the performers, stage hands, any one who might have seen her?"

"Knock yourself out." She turned back to her clipboard, lit a cigarette, and blew out a plume of smoke. She was done with me.

The so-called star of the show was a guy named Sheppard 'Shep' Breckman who was trying awfully hard to be the next Russ Columbo, a hip jazz crooner who made the ladies swoon and the men want to be just like him, except without the dramatic and mysterious death. Breckman made an effort to come across as a well-educated Ivy League man with a touch of the bootlegger in him. At least to his way of thinking. What he didn't know about gangsters could fill a library. He had a perfect haircut and an even more perfect manicure. There was oil in his voice, smooth and slippery. He made it clear in a conspiratorial way Miss Delsin was no dainty flower.

"I'll be perfectly honest with you. I tried to make her but she wouldn't tumble. She was looking for a sugar daddy to roll her in the clover. This idea of becoming a ballerina was starting to fade real fast." His hand waved off the notion in a dismissive way.

"How do you mean?"

"Malone is a task master who delivers the charm when you sign up and then cracks the whip if you don't carry your weight. You think you might get a shot at Broadway or Hollywood but the truth is we're all just grist for the mill, brother. Except me, of course. I've got connections. A couple of more months here and I'm going where the lights are shining bright. Mark my word. Hey, you can say you knew me when."

"I wish you all the luck in the world." He was

going to need a lot more than luck.

It appeared as though the first five dead women were something of a temptation, appearing as available to the killer but then perhaps something changed. The theory worked out well if you left out the laundress. My opinion was altered when we went to The Bar-B-Q Shack. From the outside it looked like a log cabin, something old settlers might have inhabited. The building was long and had tables with benches for seating and two sets of double doors in the back leading to the kitchen. The smell of smoke was imbedded into the wood. This family style restaurant was owned by the late Tangerine Smith.

No one knew what her real first name was or her exact background. According to her main cook, Shaughnessy Burkett, she presented the attitude of a Texas Guinan without the "Hello, suckers!" greeting. She had a soft spot for little kids who came in with their families for a meal of brisket and beans and corn bread and iced tea. She would occasionally put on a Southern drawl and at other times sounded like a swell from the Big Apple.

Burkett was tall and skinny with a mop of blonde hair and glasses so thick they were probably made from Coke bottles. Perhaps they hid the tears of remembrance. He was trying to show a tough front, shoulders pulled back and chest puffed out, but no one would have been put off by this wretch of a man.

"I got no idea where she come from or how she made her money before. All's I knows is she was good to everyone who worked here and everyone who et here."

"Anybody ever mad at her?" I detected a tone of

desperation in my voice.

"No, sir. Let's say a guy or gal didn't have no money to pay. She'd just say, 'Hit me up the next time.' Weren't no reason for no one to be mad at her for nothin'."

The way he told it, Tangerine Smith was a saint in a smokehouse.

The building was located up on North Lawrence Road almost out of the city limits. Tangerine was found in the back by the kitchen entrance. The report indicated the place had closed up and all the employees had left for the night. The last one to see her was a young gal named Shirley Meeks. She lived, if you could call it living, in a shack about a hundred yards from the restaurant. There was no running water or plumbing facilities and no electricity.

There was practically a shriek of fear when I rapped my knuckles on the door. The creature that opened it looked like a ghost or someone on the verge of death. Pale, sweaty, eyes red and drawn in, wearing a long sweater which completely covered her arms, and hair like a straw broom. Her lips were dry and cracked. It didn't take much to figure she was an addict of some kind. The one thing she didn't do was retreat in fear from my looks.

"Miss Meeks, we're looking into Tangerine Smith's killing. Perhaps you might know something…"

"Don't know nothin' 'bout Miss Tangerine's death." It was a reflex, not a response. She was desperate for a fix. I wasn't sure if it might help or hurt this situation.

"Where did you get your stuff?" I knew I had to be direct. Officer Roché stood as he usually did about two or three paces behind me. This gal was something he had never seen before.

Shirley looked left and right and over my shoulder, trying to be certain no one else who might be dangerous was around.

"You won't tell nobody?" I nodded my head. "Miss Tangerine took care of me. You see, I got the illness and she made sure, well, she made sure I got took care of."

"And since she's been gone you've been ill. Right?" She nodded impatiently. "Did you see anyone with Miss Tangerine the night she was killed?" She looked at me and then at Ronald and then back again. She shook her head violently. "You hear anything?" She stared straight ahead blankly, eyes wide, almost ready to pop out of her head.

"I heard her say, 'You got to go now' but I thought she was talking to me."

"Thank you, Shirley. I'm going to make sure someone comes by to help you take care of your illness."

"Thank you, sir." She disappeared inside, like a turtle withdrawing into its shell.

"What's going to happen to her?" Officer Roché asked innocently.

"Unfortunately you'll need to send a patrolman by to pick her up and bring her to the state mental hospital. The girl isn't going to make it on her own, not with Tangerine Smith dead."

It was sad when someone was too far gone they couldn't take care of themselves and had no one to take care of them. It was my own biggest fear.

Chapter Twenty-One

Ronald stared straight ahead at the road, his hands clutching the wheel as though the car was going to take over and drive on its own. I thought I saw him blinking quickly as though he might have a twitch. It was apparent he had seen and heard things over the last couple of days he could never imagine would ever be part of his life. Like the young cops in Ark City, he held a kind of vision of what it was like to be a cop, something out of a grade school reader perhaps, and so far from the realities of, well, life in general. As though everything he thought he knew about police work came from a recruitment poster. Unfortunately, I saw a lot of the same look in the war. Kids eager to be doughboys who had no earthly knowledge or understanding of death, cruel and ugly and vicious death. I guess growing up on the North Side of Chicago prepared me for more than I realized.

Detective Sells had been around quite a while. A bull like Rackler wouldn't melt like the Wicked Witch of the West. But Ronald Roché was better suited to writing parking tickets than viewing dead bodies and interviewing drug addicts and prostitutes. I had to wonder if he still wanted to be a detective.

"Would you join us for dinner, Officer Witherspoon?" Before I had a chance to inquire as to whom he meant, he continued quickly and nervously.

"My mother, well, she said you should have at least one home cooked meal while you were in town. It would be the…Christian thing to do."

Outside of Beth Handy's wedding three years ago, I hadn't been exposed to a lot of religion. I didn't begrudge anyone's worshipping in whatever fashion felt right but after going through the war, I saw Hell and I hadn't yet found anything resembling Heaven.

I would have preferred to go back to my hotel room and spend the evening going over the files and sorting through our interviews. I realized accepting his invitation was the more polite thing to do for a young man I was beginning to gather didn't have a bunch of friends.

After cleaning up a bit, I followed his directions and drove to a house on Park Place. It was one of those Victorian homes, even more fancy and elaborate than Miss Becky's place. The roof had a sharp angle. It gave off the appearance of a regal being, something placed here to oversee the rest of the sinners. Perhaps a house of the holy inhabited by the righteous.

When Ronald answered the door, he appeared far different from the young police officer who was escorting me around. His hair was combed and parted. His shirt was buttoned and the knot in his tie was perfect. His shoes were even more polished than those he wore for work. He opened the door wide to allow me entrance.

The foyer showed off an ornately carved staircase to the right, a mirror set in against a carved oak wall straight ahead, and a set of French doors to the left which opened into a parlor. The wood floors held an intricate inlaid design and were practically shining. The love seat, sofa, and two chairs had thin padding to make lounging uncomfortable after a period of time. There was a print of the Last Supper, another in sepia of Jesus with a halo, and a large ivory cross affixed above the fireplace whose hot fire was making me sweat almost instantly.

A cross above a hot fire. Heaven and Hell right here in a parlor.

Despite the wood floors and the fact she was certainly wearing shoes, the woman who entered seemed to glide, almost like a ghost appearing at will. I wasn't sure how long her hair was but it was fixed up with pins whose heads appeared to be painted enamel. The dark green velvet gown was secured tightly to her ample figure, the long sleeves reaching down to just at the wrist. Her intention may have been to cover her body but the tightness of her dress accentuated her buxom physique. What surprised me the most was her age. She appeared even younger than me. I was expecting a matronly woman, someone who had a child later in life and was perhaps overly protective. What I saw was someone who could have been Ronald Roché's older sister.

Her hand was extended toward me, and I knew enough to hold it gently in mine and place a small peck on it. I think it was Chief Taylor or his wife who had instructed me accordingly many years prior.

"Deanna Roché," she announced.

"Baron Witherspoon."

"You wear the marks of a hero, Officer Witherspoon." No one in nearly twenty years had referred to my facial scars with such an eloquent description. It was alarming as much as it was pleasing to hear.

"I thank you for your courtesy, ma'am. To be honest with you, I did nothing heroic to get these."

"But you survived. That may be the most heroic thing of all."

I couldn't disagree with her there. I survived the war. I survived Jake Hickey. I had mostly survived the notion of not being sure who I was at any given point in time.

She took my arm and guided me toward the dining room which seemed large enough to hold King Arthur and all his knights. She sat me at the head of the table while she and Ronald took seats on either side of me. I followed whatever example she set.

"Precious Lord," she intoned as we bowed our heads, my eyes sneaking a peek of her face, "we thank you for the gifts of your bounty which we enjoy at this table. As you have provided for us in the past, so you may sustain us throughout our lives. While we enjoy your gifts, may we never forget the needy and those in want." There was a brief pause but I was unwilling to get out of my prayerful pose until I was sure it was okay to do so. "So, too, give strength to men like Baron Witherspoon who, with firmness of purpose, wield your sword of justice and cleanse the world of indignity and vice. In your name we give all thanks. Amen." Ronald reiterated the salutation. I whispered it.

"I am grateful for those kind words, ma'am."

"Please do not stand on ceremony. It's Deanna."

I had many questions running through my mind but knew it was impolite to ask. Ronald's father and Deanna's husband. How she made a living and paid for all this beyond Ronald's wages. How she prepared such a large meal (roast, mashed potatoes, gravy, beets, candied carrots) all without any house staff. What she did to occupy her days and nights. She intrigued me and fascinated me in just a brief period of time.

My purpose in Wichita was to assist the police department in the investigation of a series of brutal murders. These thoughts of Ronald Roché and his mother were passing distractions, notions to pull me away from the fact I was really doing no good and would not be taken seriously.

After the meal, Ronald took the dishes to the kitchen while Deanna guided me back to the parlor. It started to feel somewhat uncomfortable sitting there with her on the love seat and realizing we were about the same age. She had the same ethereal quality Natalie Dixon had when I first met her as well, only there was a peaceful feeling. Right now, I just wanted to leave, and I couldn't determine exactly what caused this discomfort.

"Might I?" Deanna raised her hand and held it several inches away from my face. "Touch your marks?" She would not say the word 'scars' as though it were an offense. I had no idea why she would be so fascinated by these lines in my face, pale pink, often tight and on occasion, depending on the weather, with a tingling feeling. I nodded to indicate my approval.

Her forefinger delicately traced the lines from forehead, down the cheeks, and across my chin. She looked at the scars themselves, not my face, not into my eyes, as though there were ancient hieroglyphics inscribed, some kind of code or symbol my face represented, perhaps a message from the one she worshipped.

The sound of Ronald coming out from the kitchen into the dining room startled her for a moment and caused her to stop abruptly.

"I regret we have no sherry to offer you. We do not consume alcohol in this house."

"Plus, there's still Prohibition in Kansas," Ronald chimed in.

"That's quite all right, ma'am," I said in defiance of her earlier edict. "Besides, I best be going. Still much work to be done." She had a look of pride, more than the kind mothers have for their children. "Ronald, I'll be getting to the station house earlier than you. I'll use the empty office you first brought me to."

Deanna Roché stood up and escorted me to the door. Her gaze turned toward mine, her eyes searching now. Maybe she was still looking at the scars. She opened the door for me, then held both my hands.

"May the Lord keep and protect you, Baron."

She leaned in and pressed her lips lightly to both of my cheeks. I moved softly toward the door and in doing so pulled my hands from hers. This was the most normal place I had visited in the last two days which really wasn't saying much.

Chapter Twenty-Two

I don't know if I didn't get much sleep because I was eager to get to the station or if something else was bothering me. It was the city and its ways churning around in my head. Rather funny to consider I grew up in Chicago, in the middle of the Windy City, hunkering down with other Irish toughs, before going off to the war. For nearly twenty years, small town life had settled on me like a warm woolen coat, comforting and snug, so much so the city now felt like an enemy. Time changes you along with your memories.

Mornings at the police station in Ark City were usually quiet. There was very little crime to speak of and not as many officers as bigger cities. If I felt like going in early to catch up on paperwork or read reports from other areas, I could do it in peace. Perhaps I was expecting such peace in Wichita but it wasn't to be.

If it weren't for the privacy of the unused office, I would have been distracted by all the commotion from the officers and other personnel continually passing through the corridors. The fact they were unaware of this office made it fortunate for me. I could see the shadows of bodies but did my best to focus on the reports and my notes from the previous two days.

My process was the same as it was in Ark City, back when three men were brutally murdered: identify similarities and patterns and try to create an image of the perpetrator. The women were vastly different. The first victim, Jessica Rabal, was a petite blonde who worked as a laundress. Found in the alley behind the establishment. Completely different from any of the other victims. Perhaps the killer was learning how to kill. Chantelle Boudreau was from New Orleans, possible Cajun or Creole. Angela Ramirez was Mexican. Aurora Chao was Asian, thought to be Chinese. They were prostitutes. Valeria Delsin was a Russian émigré and a dancer. Tangerine Smith was a white woman in her late thirties where the other five were in their early twenties. She ran a restaurant and took care of those in need even if doing so meant breaking the law. There was really nothing to tie these six women together.

All of the victims were stabbed in the abdomen. The penetrations were deep and in three of the five there were what appeared to be tearing wounds as though the object were slicing upward or sideways. Based on the location of the point of entry and the heights of the women, the perpetrator was calculated to be roughly five foot six inches to five foot nine inches. A great amount of strength was not required based on the type of wound. However, the perpetrator would have had to get close enough to the women. In this regard, all six were of a trusting enough nature, either by profession or disposition, to allow such closeness.

A nice guy approaches a woman, then stabs her with a resolute thrust in the belly, perhaps silences her with a hand over her mouth, and keeps pushing his blade in deeper until the victim passes out from loss of blood. A height and a personality. That's all I had. It was still necessary to figure out why.

It was approaching nine in the morning. I had gotten here slightly before six. Nearly three hours without food or coffee and my head was spinning. I needed Dr. Brenz to listen to what I had and make some order of it but he was in Ark City. Some coffee would have to be the next best thing.

Sells and Rackler were at their desk in the detectives' room, heads down and buried in files; they looked up when I entered.

"So, who's the killer, buddy?" I could count on Rackler to play the role of stagecoach driver, whipping the horses in a frenzy to make them go faster.

"You have anything?" Sells was more matter-of-fact, trying to keep it as professional as possible even though I knew he didn't like me almost as much as Rackler.

"Yeah. The killer is a nice guy with a big smile." I kept the same matter-of-fact tone, saying the words as though they were a new revelation. They couldn't be sure if I were joking or actually had some strange notion. Rackler's eyebrows tightened into what passed for an attempt at thought, and his mouth was open and slack jawed. Whatever he was trying to say didn't make it out.

"What makes you say so?" Sells was driving the stagecoach now, keeping everything at a steady gallop.

"The killings are not vicious and wild. They're calm."

"You think someone who's calm kills women like that?" Rackler had only one train of thought: he was a better cop than me.

"Yes. I've seen killings where there were multiple stab wounds, blood all over the victim's clothing. All of these murders were initiated from a single entry wound. That takes someone who is calm and controlled."

"You saying this guy is not a raving lunatic?" Rackler's lack of experience was showing. Sells wasn't going to stop his partner from looking like a fool. It was certainly one way to learn, perhaps the best way.

I took measured steps and approached Rackler, a smile on my face, my arms down by my side. He squinted, trying to look past my scars, into my eyes, and clear through to my intentions. The problem was he was intellectually blind.

"I'm not a raving lunatic and I just got close enough to stick a bayonet into your belly." He looked down and saw a letter opener in my right hand before jumping backward. I turned back to Sells, in part to let Rackler know I wasn't going to actually assault him. Sells had a smirk on his face. Seems like Rackler would have several teachers.

"None of these women, not even the prostitutes, are going to let a raving lunatic approach them. This killer is warm and charming, maybe even sweet, possibly younger. I don't know. But he looks normal, whatever that means."

"Like you?" Rackler was still three or four feet behind me but it sounded as though he had whispered in my ear. I turned suddenly, sharply, this time my gaze locked on his like a bloodhound finds a coon.

"No, Detective Rackler. I certainly don't look normal. If I weren't wearing a uniform, there is hardly any female who would let me get intimately close to them. No, our murderer is as charming as, well, you."

My face was cold as stone and as blank. We stood staring at each other for what seemed like forever. The thing was I had already experienced forever and I could take it.

"John, you got anything relevant to say?" Sells was trying to give me a chance and keep his partner from starting an unwarranted fight. Rackler sat back down at his desk, looked up at me, and pouted. "Yeah, that's what I thought." Sells looked back to me. "All right, you got a nice guy with a smile. What's his name? Where does he live? What does he do for a living?"

What Detective Sells did right there was to take all my hard work and evaluating and throw it into a trash basket. He and Rackler didn't care for motivations or character types. They needed hard facts, answers to one simple question: Who had killed six women? I couldn't blame them for their attitude because I understood them. Someone thought I had all this special knowledge and amazing skills and I was going to walk in and point to someone on the streets of Wichita and say, "There's your man" and then everyone would be happy. I was alone in the big city, completely out of my element, with only my instinct and will to live and survive.

"We figured out this much, we'll figure out the rest." I was being gracious by saying 'we' but it didn't seem to matter.

"Well, until then," Sells continued "he's still out there killing."

Sells asked the question any cop would ask but did so without even acknowledging this analysis made sense or could be useful. As far as I was concerned, I could have spent another day driving around the city, stopped off at a restaurant for a good steak, and driven home, leaving guys like Sells and Rackler to wallow in their own pig sty. But I was a cop, too. My hope was they would eventually see I wasn't the enemy.

Ronald Roché walked in right after Sells comments. It almost seemed to me as though he were just outside waiting for the right time to step in because his timing was impeccable. He surveyed the scene, from me to Sells to Rackler and back to me.

"The chief wishes to see you, Officer Witherspoon." I looked at Sells waiting to see if there would be any acknowledgement, any consideration for my efforts. I thought he might be the one to actually recognize what it meant. In the end, he was just an old guy wanting to walk off into the sunset all on his own. The scary thought was I might wind up insignificant as well.

Ronald's walk was stiff, almost military, the utter professional. Perhaps it was going to the police chief's office that made his spine stiff.

Chief Wilson was signing several papers, placing them on the blotter, and creating a neat and stacked pile. After I entered his office, he placed his pen down carefully, and looked up at me, the fingertips of both hands evenly placed against each other almost in prayer. His invocation was short of the mark.

"Officer Witherspoon, I want to thank you for taking the time to come up from Arkansas City and offer us your perspective on this case. We appreciate your efforts and are grateful for your insight."

"Sir?"

"I've spoken with Bert Wells, the City Manager, and Dr. Weaver, the mayor. They are now of the belief we will be able to proceed with this investigation on our own."

Ark City wasn't the only place where politics was a

game played by men in suits seated behind big desks. A slight smile came upon my face. I wanted to chuckle as much as I did watching *Bringing Up Baby* with Cary Grant and Katherine Hepburn. I wanted to have a pain in my belly from laughing so hard thinking a killer was going to keep on with his path, his mission, and none of these cops were going to ever find him unless they got lucky.

But I didn't. I just smiled, and nodded, and turned to leave the office. Ronald Roché escorted me as far as the main entrance.

"I'm sorry to see you go. I learned a lot from you." His comments seemed sincere. I didn't know what to say in return. Two days of putting in my best efforts on someone else's behalf and being turned away like a beggar. It was time to go home.

Chapter Twenty-Three

Somehow the drive seemed longer going back to Ark City. Two days in Wichita, the Peerless Princess of the Plains, and I was sent home about as fast and unexpectedly as I was called upon. I didn't see the purpose to begin with but once I was there it was my obligation to help in any and every way I could. Former councilman Hallett had nothing to do with this but I reckoned it was just as dirty. Why not? Wichita was a much bigger city with far more politicians and obviously a lot more dirt lying around.

There was no possible way Sells and Rackler were going to solve this case, certainly not with their current attitudes. Sells seemed like he was ready to retire and was looking for either a resolution to this case to put a feather in his cap or for time to run out and allow him to walk away. Rackler was a brute who didn't have much thought for the motivations of others. He was like an angry bull in a pasture surrounded by a rickety fence. Admittedly, I was no genius in this field but I had figured out about Natalie Dixon by the same process. Given the time and their cooperation, the answer might have appeared.

I got back to the station shortly after noon. I had neither breakfast nor lunch and it was nothing more than anger fueling me. I wasn't sure what I was supposed to do. The Arkansas City police department didn't often "loan out" an officer. There was no actual procedure written down anywhere. When Dave Morton saw me and told me to report to the chief, it was as though a protocol was being created on the spot.

Chief Richardson was still on the phone but waved me in. His expression was of a bloodhound that had been run through the county and was now plum tired. There were a few nods and "uh-huh" thrown in but it was evident he was listening as he was supposed to. After a bit he hung up.

"Officer Witherspoon…" He pinched the top of his nose, his fingers digging in to the corners of his eyes. "Baron, I'm sorry. Truly I am. It seems this was all an issue—"

"I understand, sir." I did. I knew how elected officials acted and believed their opinions were irrefutable. Wichita was the biggest city around so their problems were magnified. Drawing me into the picture only made us look like backwoods idiots. That, more than anything, rattled Chief Richardson's nerves.

"Take the rest of the day off. File a report tomorrow. Turn your receipts into the comptroller for reimbursement."

"Sir, I think I—"

"You're done with this case, Baron. You're done with Wichita."

He looked at me, more like stared at me, trying not to be upset because this wasn't ours to deal with despite him knowing how much I would grab on to a case and shake it until something fell out. This wasn't our case, his eyes seemed to reiterate. I nodded and walked out, knowing I would be heading directly over to the *Traveler* offices to visit Sandy Clevenger.

Typing up reports one click of the typewriter at a time, Sandy almost looked like she was ready to fall asleep or perhaps was actually doing her work in her sleep. I wasn't going to let my foul mood get in the way of what I knew was going to be an infectious smile.

"Professor Clevenger," I intoned and before long her head popped up, saw me, and there was her famous smile.

"Why, Baron Witherspoon, what brings you to my humble classroom?"

"Need some research on something, well, pretty nasty and gruesome."

She leaned over the typewriter trying to get as close to where I was leaning over the counter. We were like a vaudeville version of Bonnie and Clyde.

"I like it so far."

"I need you to look through back editions for cases of multiple murders in the same jurisdiction. Stabbings. Women more than men. Unsolved cases."

"Kansas?"

"National. Or…"

"Or?"

"International."

She raised her eyebrow in a suspicious way. Last time I asked for her help, it was for the local killings. I hadn't asked her anything like it since. While I was disappointed I hadn't been able to liven up her days, I was grateful we didn't have these kinds of killings here.

"This have to do with Wichita?"

"How did you know I was up there?"

"I didn't 'til now. But it's been in the paper."

I leaned in closer as well, sharing a conspiratorial attitude.

"What do you make of it?"

"Reminds me of the notorious case in England fifty years ago. The Whitechapel murders."

"Don't suppose anyone from the case is still alive?"

"I doubt it. Why?"

"I've got some ideas about the Wichita killings. Only I'm not on their force and I'm not part of their case. I just need to find someone to talk with who might, I don't know, give me some kind of direction."

She reached out and patted my hand.

"Aren't you ever going to settle down and give up all this foolishness?"

I got a lump in my throat, not because the sentiment was touching but because I had to stop myself from getting angry with her. The sentiment got me riled up more than the lady.

"See what you can find."

I left quickly. It dawned on me she was right. There was one hope for me to experience something normal, whatever the word was supposed to mean, and it was Natalie Dixon. I had been so desperate for love and affection I would have been willing to hide her crimes if only we could have been together. After her death, it didn't much seem like there was anything else for me. I ran away from being Eric Kimble, Chicago gangster. I hid from being Eric Kimble, soldier. I took the identity of Baron Witherspoon, Kansas farm boy turned police officer. I was a combination of two people which didn't make me better or greater or more fulfilled. I was a new being who really had no past and could not see any kind of a future.

So I continued on being a police officer, seeking

out bad people and trying to stop them. It would probably go on like this until I just died, either by a criminal's gun or from some natural malady. Convincing myself this is what I was good at gave me all the motivation I needed. Everything else people thought I should have, like a loving wife and a house with a picket fence, was someone else's dreams. I only had nightmares.

Chapter Twenty-Four

Weeks passed. There were the usual drunks brought in to sleep it off and a few kids itching to get out of school for the summer who were causing general mayhem. There were no gangsters from the big city, at least none we knew of. There were no horrific murders, and that was for certain. It was the Ark City everyone had always known. And it started to bore me.

I realized a part of me was still Eric Kimble, the part itching to rebel against the tried-and-true life of Baron Witherspoon. Maybe the reason I was so upset at being sent home from Wichita was because I was so excited to be involved in such a case. I felt alive in the midst of death. It occurred to me I had become who I am now as far back as the war. Fear and imminent death gave me a purpose.

Dave Morton offered to fix me up on a double date with the older of the two Grier sisters. However, she turned out to be a little bit more of a Bible thumper than I wanted to be around. It got me to thinking about Deanna Roché and how I didn't think of her in the same way. The buxom figure stuck out more in my mind and in more of the right places.

Just when I had forgotten about my request, Sandy Clevenger stomped into the police station with a thick stack of newspapers. She had a mischievous smile on her face, definitely like a feral cat that had caught a field mouse. I escorted her to an unused office, similar to the one I used in Wichita. Blood started to flow rapidly through my body.

"Well, of course we talked about the Whitechapel Killer. Then there was some fella called H.H. Holmes in Chicago about the time of the World's Fair back in '93. There was a French guy, Joseph Vacher. Not sure if I'm pronouncing it right. They called him the 'French Ripper'."

All the while, she was filing through her stack of newspapers to show me the articles. They were mostly notices of their execution and less about the actual case.

"Anything more recent?"

"The Germans seemed to have had their hands full. This one guy, Fritz Haarmann, was called 'The Butcher of Hanover' and this other guy, Peter Kurten, was known as 'The Vampire of Dusseldorf.' Pretty gruesome, huh? At least they gave them good nicknames, right?" Her smile was no indication of any kind of disgust. It was more like watching a Three Stooges short at the movies. "First one was executed in '25 and the second in '31."

It wasn't my intention to show my disappointment but the whole idea of this was to reach out to the investigators to get a better understanding of their case. I didn't speak German and telegrams back and forth weren't going to get me any clearer picture. Making sure I explained this specifically to Sandy and not blaming her, she held up a hand as though to stop me from seeing her off.

"We got this other one. They call him the 'Mad Butcher of Kingsbury Run' and it's right up in Cleveland. They speak English there, right?" I smirked at her and read the paper from just this past April. The thing that struck me like lightning was the communications from the police to the press were made by Eliot Ness who at the time was the Public Safety Director of Cleveland. It wasn't easy to tell if he was in charge of the case or merely just the mouthpiece. Nevertheless, this was a man whose reputation carried weight. I was certain to be able to get the kind of direction I was seeking.

My first task was to reach out to him. I needed to do so in an official capacity so he wouldn't take me for an autograph seeker. The call would have to come directly from the department. I walked Sandy out as I headed for the switchboard operator, Linda Kuchenberg. She was always dolled up with her hair in an elegant bun and was made up as though every day were Friday night, never bemoaning her spinster status.

"You coming over for dinner on Sunday?" Sandy asked her as she passed.

"Only if you're making a roast." Sandy smiled and left. I looked at Linda, to the front door where Sandy had just passed, and back to Linda.

"I didn't know you knew Sandy."

"She's my sister. Hmm…some detective you are." All I could do was shake my head.

"I need you to contact the Cleveland Department of Public Safety. Try to get hold of Eliot Ness. Tell him one of the officers here is investigating a case similar to the Kingsbury Run butcher."

"Sure, Baron. How long do you want me to try?"

"Until you get a hold of him."

As I walked back to my desk, I realized how involved I was in this case and I didn't know why.

Maybe it was to make up for Natalie or even Heather Devore. Jake Hickey had come into town and threatened to undermine the lives of a lot of good people. His desperation got his lady killed, and he wound up getting his head blown off. I don't say it was because of me. Jake was going to act as he always had. Natalie was on a personal quest. I just got in the way of both. This was one case where I might have a say in the outcome instead of just being in the crowd watching the show.

More than that was the notion of something to do and, along with it, someone to be. I had lost my way, feeling like I was caught in a twister just spinning me round, not knowing where I'd land until I landed.

The case files were no longer available to me but I still had all my personal notes. I had read the newspaper every single day since I got back and didn't find any further articles about the killings in Wichita. It could have meant they ended altogether or the killer recognized the investigation was heating up and decided to stop for a bit. It made a certain degree of sense considering I felt the perpetrator was on a personal mission, somewhat like Natalie. Then I changed my mind and decided someone so driven would not be capable of stopping but needed to see it through to the end. On the other hand—

Miss Banister called me to the kitchen when I got home and served up a slice of chocolate zucchini bread and poured me a cup of very hot black coffee. She had me sit with her at the breakfast nook while she sipped her tea. If I didn't know any better, I would have sworn she was an English lady with her grace and charm.

"You've been distant," she said calmly.

"More so than usual?" I tried to divert her with humor but no one had ever accused me of being a funny guy.

"You should find a nice girl and settle down. I think it would be better for you."

"I don't know much else besides being a policeman. Wasn't much good at farming. To be honest with you, Miss Banister, I really can't see me all nice and cozy behind some white picket fence with a wife and some kids and a dog. It works well for most folks but not for me."

I sipped my coffee. The richness of the cake made me feel like a king. Miss Banister had her delightful smile, looking like a kitten before it pounced, and said, "I think it's time to stop running away."

Just like Dr. Brenz, I could never tell if she knew more than she admitted. But I was so far removed from the past I had to stop caring about it reaching up from the grave and dragging me down.

The door knocker hit viciously and repeatedly against wood. My instincts took over, and I sprinted to the front door, holding one hand behind me to ward Miss Banister away. Dave Morton stood on the step panting as though he had run all the way from Tulsa.

"Linda Kuchenberg's got Eliot Ness on the phone."

Chapter Twenty-Five

It was a French forest somewhere. The squadron leader was Corporal Baron Witherspoon who had taken over after Staff Sergeant Frieberg had been killed by a sniper. He led us toward what he had been told was a foxhole with a German machine gun unit. A shell exploded over our collective left shoulders. We spun around like tops, eyes bugging out of our heads. We thought we were headed in the wrong direction. So we did what anyone would do which was to run away from the shelling. Until they started coming from in front of us. Caught in a crossfire and needing to find a way out, Cpl. Witherspoon led us in a diagonal path away from the intersecting shells. There was a trench about fifty yards in front of us. Witherspoon stopped and pushed each of us past him. I fell. He picked me up. The shelling was right behind us. I ran faster than I ever had. Faster than running from the cops after roughing up a news vendor. Witherspoon had to push me as I was faltering. I fell in just as a shell exploded right behind him, pushing him forward, pushing him on top of me.

I ran almost as fast back to the station house realizing it had been twenty years since that happened. I let Eric Kimble die in the war and brought Baron Witherspoon back to life. Brought him back home.

Linda Kuchenberg saw my sweaty red face and probably thought she needed to call the undertaker. I did everything I could to quickly catch my breath before panting "I'll be in the records room." It was similar to the large room at the Cowley County Courthouse but with far fewer file cabinets, a small table and uncomfortable wooden chair, and a phone. Very rarely was it used by anyone except detectives.

I couldn't be sure how I was going to sound after running so fast and so hard. After all, this was the man who created The Untouchables and brought down Capone, something George 'Bugs' Moran and 'Crazy' Jake Hickey could never do. It was important to impress him as a police officer.

"Mr. Ness, thank you so much for returning my calls."

"I'm sorry for the delay, Officer Witherspoon. Weren't sure who you were until I had you looked up. You brought down Jake Hickey."

"Well, it wasn't just me…"

"I understand. People think I brought Capone down all by myself." There was an awkward pause, like I had just met a movie star at a gala and didn't have anything worthwhile to say other than admitting being a fan. "What can I do for you?"

"I was asked to consult on a case in Wichita seems to have some similarities to a case you've been working on."

"The torso killer."

"Yes." There was another pause. The silence had me concerned he might not be willing to assist.

"You say you were asked to consult on this case?"

"Correct, sir."

"And are you still consulting?"

"The detectives on the case decided to follow a

different lead than the course of my investigation." I don't know where such a sentence came from but it was the smartest thing I had ever said in my life. I also wasn't sure how it would play out. "I'm certain, with your guidance, I could bring this case to some closure and assist them in getting an arrest."

"I see." I heard papers rattle and maybe what sounded like his fingers strumming on a blotter pad. "I'd be happy to show you around our case. You might pick something up. Plus, we could also use a fresh set of eyes. Could be beneficial for both of us."

I had hoped to discuss this over the phone or perhaps have him send me some files. Going to Cleveland was not what I had planned. Then again, I wasn't sure what I had planned. You read Eliot Ness is involved in a major case and you reach out to him for guidance and he invites you into his home, so to speak. It was time to follow a new road.

"It would be an honor, sir. I'll let you know when I've made arrangements."

The feeling of satisfaction I expected to have after talking with a law enforcement legend like Eliot Ness was soured by the confusing notion of having to make my way to Cleveland to get help investigating a case with which I was no longer involved. It certainly didn't make any sense. However, it was an opportunity I could not overlook.

Heading to Chief Richardson's office, I tried rehearsing various lines in my mind but none of them sounded as smart as I just did with Ness. Maybe I was only good for one intelligent line per day. It was made perfectly clear to me why I had been requested by the Wichita Police Department as well as why I was asked to leave. This was more about image to them than solving the case. The brotherhood of police was closing ranks and leaving one of their own, me, out.

"I have an opportunity to consult with Eliot Ness regarding the killings in Wichita. It might wind up being a great learning experience for our department as well." I stood at attention, just like Cpl. Witherspoon.

"You're no longer on the Wichita case, Officer Witherspoon."

"Sir, Mr. Ness is a highly respected—"

"I know who Eliot Ness is."

"Yes, sir."

I could feel this chance slipping away. To be honest, I had no idea why it was so important to me. Maybe the lack of respect I received from fellow police officers in another city drove me to prove something. It might have been nothing more than the notion of growing older and not having anything to show for my forty years on this earth. When all is said and done, a man wants to point to something, one thing, and say, "I did it. That thing, it was because of me. And it was good."

"I've been noticing in your files you haven't taken a vacation since you started on the force. Close to twenty years and never having a vacation. Remarkable."

"Yes, sir."

"I think you're due for a couple of weeks off with pay."

"It would be greatly appreciated, sir."

"Your vacation begins today."

His head dropped down and continued looking through reports. He didn't have a chance to see my smile. I turned to leave, my hand on the door knob, when I heard him speak.

"Baron."

"Yes, sir?" I said turning back.

"Come back with something." His eyes seemed hopeful. I nodded in agreement and left.

Chapter Twenty-Six

Time and money.

Those were valuable things, not just to gangsters but to the every day working-class guy. It never seemed there was enough of either. A gangster knew he wouldn't have the time but could get the money. The mill worker or factory worker or farmer had nothing but time yet very little money to show for it. Perhaps we were all looking in the wrong direction.

I made $1333 per year, just a little over $25 a week. I was sure unlikely to spend a week and a half's pay on first class train fare. I took a local to Joplin out of Ark City which mostly carried grain and was then able to catch a Missouri railroad to Kansas City. From there, I traveled to Chicago and then over to Cleveland. It took me nearly a whole day but only $15 total because I sat in the worst seats possible. It was probably better because people in those seats really don't care what you look like as much as the ritzy swells in First Class. My thought was even if I had spent good cabbage they would have tossed me out based on some obscure and unstated rule. I was where I needed to be.

I had a three-hour layover in Union Station in Chicago. It was barely four miles from the SMC Cartage building where nine years earlier the fate of the North Side Gang and Jake Hickey was set forever.

What would have happened, I thought, if Dion O'Banion hadn't encouraged me to go off to war? The possibilities were endless. I could have been killed either by the South Siders or by 'Crazy' Jake himself. I might have been on the receiving end of a Valentines card from Capone. I could be in jail or successfully running my own gang, rolling in the dough, a good-looking wife and kids and myself with a good looking face. As it was, this scarred vet was on his way to a meeting with the man who had brought Capone down. The irony was as thick as a fall fog in the Windy City.

A clerk at the station said I could save cab fare by walking to the City Hall where the Public Safety Director's Office was located. I walked down East 9th and turned onto Lakeside Avenue. It was the biggest public building I had ever seen, even bigger than anything in Wichita. It made me believe their police force was far more superior to anything I had been aware of before. Then again, they were investigating a series of grisly murders no one seemed to be able to figure out. The size of the building made no difference.

Several guards directed me to the proper wing of the building. Not one reacted to my facial scars with the slightest degree of disgust or anguish. It made me angry the police officers in Wichita had treated me with such contempt. Then it dawned on me their attitude was based on my intelligence and not my appearance.

The outside door read Director of Public Safety. An attractive redheaded secretary typed up reports when I tapped lightly on the door and walked in. She looked up and her emerald green eyes glistened almost as brightly as her moist red lipstick. Her blouse seemed a bit too small as her bosom pushed snuggly against it.

Like the policemen I encountered so far, she smiled at me, neither afraid nor concerned. She was in a legitimate line of work but far more tantalizing than Heather Devore.

"I'm here to see Mr. Ness."

"Is he is expecting you?"

"I believe so."

"Who should I say is calling on him?"

"Baron Witherspoon. Officer Baron Witherspoon from Arkansas City, Kansas."

"Officer Baron Witherspoon." She emphasized my title as though impressed and then picked up the phone and dialed one number. She looked up at me once or twice as she spoke. Her tongue glided across her lower lip. I was really enjoying Cleveland so far.

"He'll see you now, Officer Witherspoon." I couldn't help but smile.

Ness was well groomed and well dressed, a dapper figure who met my expectation of him by virtue of his reputation. He stood from behind his desk and came out in front of it to warmly shake my hand. I dropped my satchel to the floor beside me.

"Glad you could make it, Baron. You just got in?"

"Yes, sir."

"If I'm not mistaken, you're about five years older than me. Why don't you drop the 'sir' and just call me Eliot?" I nodded. I couldn't have felt more relaxed and at ease if I had tried.

"I'm really impressed," I said, unconsciously looking back over my shoulder.

"Miss Hammersmith? Yes, isn't she a peach? But you haven't come all this way to look at our delectable office personnel. Why don't you have a seat and tell me about your case."

I sat in a comfortable leather chair opposite him and started to relate the Wichita murders to him. I backtracked at one point to describe my investigation of the three murders in Ark City back in '35, leaving out the part about Natalie Dixon. He had Miss Hammersmith bring in a tray with a carafe of coffee and two cups. Our gazes met again, and hers seemed very inviting.

"I like your approach to both of these cases. The notion of scientific policing and using psychological analysis is the way to go. I think it will be the future of law enforcement."

"I think so, too. I just can't get the Wichita police department to see."

"You have to understand, Baron, there's more to fighting crime than just going after the bad guys. Do you have any idea what I had to deal with in Chicago? It's the reason we created The Untouchables. And then when I started here, it was even worse, if you can imagine. But we got a Grand Jury two years ago. Fifteen city officials, two captains, two lieutenants, and a sergeant. All of them, gone. Two hundred police officers were forced to turn in their resignations. Once you get rid of the bad apples you can plant a whole new orchard."

I liked the sound of that. I liked him and his enthusiasm. Falling into another man's skin and following the course of his life had been my fresh start, my new orchard. But I had little opportunity for anything more. The chance to work on a case in Wichita gave me the hope of expanding my horizons but only ended up as a closed door. There was a passing thought I should move up here, work alongside Eliot Ness and make a real name for myself.

"Could I see your files on the torso case?"

"Absolutely. We can head on over to the police department and talk to a couple of detectives."

"You mean you're not investigating directly?"

"I just coordinate the investigations. It's not like the old days. Come on. We'll walk. It's just a block away. Plus, it's not so hot for August. You can leave your bag here." He grabbed his hat and briskly walked past me and toward the door. "Miss Hammersmith, hold all my calls."

The alluring redhead looked at me with a gracious smile.

"It was a pleasure meeting you, Officer Witherspoon."

"And you, miss. I'll be here for several days, I imagine." I have no idea where those words came from. It had been happening a lot lately.

"How delightful."

This was certainly a perk of law enforcement.

Chapter Twenty-Seven

I must have had a faraway look on my face, something dreamy and distant. Ness tapped me on the shoulder.

"A dish like her can get you in some serious trouble. I know. I'm on the outs with my wife because of her."

"You're having an affair?" There was disappointment in my voice as though the possibilities of a roll in the hay were being nixed.

"No, nothing of the sort. It's just that I work a lot. All the time really. And my wife can't help but think there is something amiss. She thinks she's some kind of detective." He smiled but prevented himself from outright laughing. "The truth is there isn't anything going on, but there were a few thoughts every once in a blue moon." His smile remained but it didn't seem as genuine now. "She doesn't like it when I have a drink with some of the guys at the office either. Says it isn't right for a former Prohibition agent to be drinking even though Prohibition is over. Come to think of it, she doesn't approve of a lot of things I do." He was a man who knew his limitations which made me respect him even more.

We got to police headquarters which rivaled the City Hall building as the most magnificent thing I had seen. Ness walked through the front doors, into the main lobby, greeting many people along the way. He seemed genuinely liked. Perhaps his reputation had been carried from Chicago and maintained along the way.

Taking the stairs two at a time, we were up on the second floor in a sprint and then down a long hallway to the detectives' room. Unlike Wichita, this seemed to span four or five offices worth of space. There were perhaps twenty desks, each with a phone and two baskets for files. A chalk board at the very far wall filled with columns indicated outstanding cases. At the top were the words Kingsbury Run.

Ness brought us over to a far corner where two detectives were busy at work. "Detectives Lindsay and Gallison," Ness announced, "this is Officer Baron Witherspoon from Arkansas City, Kansas." Both of their handshakes were warm and firm. Their eyes never wavered from my face. Detective Lindsay seemed like a taller version of Ness with a pencil thin moustache and pince-nez glasses. He looked more like a college professor than an experienced law enforcement officer. Detective Gallison was a big man, equally tall, broad shoulders barely fitting inside his jacket, but with kind eyes. He had dark black hair. It was the only thing from keeping him looking like Santa Claus. "Detectives Peter Merylo and Martin Zalewski are the primary detectives," he said to me, "but they keep running into dead ends. These guys are my back ups, only the chief and commissioner don't know it." There were knowing smiles between the three of them. He turned back to Lindsay and Gallison. "We're trading sets of eyes. His look at our case. Ours look at his."

"Seems fair enough." Gallison pulled up a third

chair. Ness indicated he had rounds to make.

"You fellas okay with being backups?" I felt like the simple-minded college freshman, unaware of how things worked.

"Not a problem." Gallison's baritone voice was actually soothing. "We're not trying to win any awards. Just catch a killer."

I sat there with these two professionals while we went over everything they had on what the press was calling the Mad Butcher of Kingsbury Run. There had been a disparity between the finding of bodies and the actual time of each murder as determined by scientific methods. Only two of the ten victims had been identified. There were decapitations with some of the heads having never been recovered. Two of the male victims had been emasculated. One of the John Does, dubbed The Tattooed Man, was determined to have been decapitated while still alive. Three women, seven men. One black victim.

"This one is particularly interesting," Lindsay said while showing me the file. "It's from just this past April. A part of the victim's lower leg was recovered. Less than a month later, May second, a human thigh was found in the Cuyahoga River in the Cleveland Flats just east of the West 3rd Street Bridge. We searched under the bridge and discovered a burlap sack, the kind you can purchase at any dry goods store. It contained a headless torso cut in half, another thigh, and a left foot. Thus far, we have not found a head or any remaining body parts. Additionally, it is the only victim found with drugs in her system."

"What kind of drugs?" This was all new to me.

"According to the file, Samuel Gerber, the medical

examiner, says it was some kind of narcotic, possibly in the opioid family."

"It doesn't make sense. If torture and suffering are the goal, why dull the pain? Why make it easier?" I could feel my mind working like it did three years ago and then again when I was in Wichita. My thought processes were sharp, perhaps to fight off the concerns I had battling my own sense of identity.

"Nothing about this case makes sense," Gallison chimed in. "When you look at all the files, ten of them so far, you say this is the work of a mad man, a complete lunatic. Right? Then you consider the time and effort involved to do this and you realize it takes precision and skill. So, it doesn't add up to a lunatic."

"You said 'so far?' Do you think—?"

"I think he's going to continue until he's caught or killed. He likes it. He's getting good at it. Unless—"

"Unless what?" I felt like I was waiting for the punch line to a joke.

"Well, maybe he thinks he's on some kind of mission and now he's finally done. But I don't think we're gonna get that lucky."

I nodded because I understood and agreed. It was the same thing as in Wichita although different circumstances. A pattern develops. Maybe it's like a chess game or a jigsaw puzzle. There are pieces put into place by the perpetrator. The job of the detective is to figure out how and why they go together.

"Ness thinks he has a suspect." Lindsay was sounding hopeful.

"Ness is good at cleaning up corruption and lowering traffic fatalities. I've heard his theories on this one and they just don't add up." I looked at Gallison inquisitively. "Ness had us conduct an interview with a Dr. Francis Sweeney. Figured it had to be a medical man given the nature of the killings. Sounded okay by me. A guy named Emil Fronek claimed the doctor tried to drug him several years ago. The interview and the investigation didn't quite pan out."

"But now he thinks the killer could be either hiding or living in the shanty town around Kingsbury Run," Lindsay added.

"Look, Officer Witherspoon, I don't mean to sound negative." Gallison had the tone of St. Nick in his voice, loving and giving. "Mr. Ness is under a lot of pressure. They brought him here to find this monster and it's been a bumpy go along the way. Us old timers don't like chasing bad leads. On the other hand, we've got to go anywhere there might be a crack of light."

I had been in town for four hours and had learned more about Eliot Ness and police work than I expected. It all made sense with him working as much as he did, having someone as alluring as Miss Hammersmith being a distraction, a distrusting wife, and a lot of hair brained theories in the hope of finding a killer. The difference between Cleveland and Wichita was this city was willing to unlock every door even if it led nowhere. Perhaps desperation was the driving force. Perhaps Wichita would get desperate one day.

Chapter Twenty-Eight

I was able to get a room a block away with the assistance of the detectives who freely threw Eliot's name around. It was as though the landlady couldn't do enough for me despite making very little eye contact. She was the first person I encountered in Cleveland who had an issue with my facial scars. My dream world was brought back into reality. To some, I was still a monster, or at the very least someone to approach with caution.

After finding a diner for a hearty breakfast, I made my way back to the police building and went over all the files with Lindsay and Gallison. I decided to review them without further input in order to come up with a conclusion all my own and see how it matched theirs. The disappointing thing was everything I considered was parallel with their analysis. We contemplated a person with some medical knowledge or, in fact, an actual butcher. The process of dismemberment required time and an ideal location, perhaps a house with a basement or an abandoned building such as were to be found in the Kingsbury Run area. We removed the notion of 'madness' assuming the perpetrator to be mentally unstable or insane. However, a full-blown lunatic would not have the capability to maintain the sense of control necessary to complete such a gory business. After several hours of review and conversation, we met at the same point and it led to a brick wall.

They proceeded to inquire about the case in Wichita. It was a slower process considering I had no files or pictures to show them and could only go by the notes I had taken and later had transcribed. Lindsay described what he felt was either an element of justice or moral rectitude based on the victims. When I pointed out Tangerine Smith seemed to be a giving and loving person and Jessica Rabal had no connection to the prostitutes, Lindsay indicated perspective was the key to understanding his point.

"It's never how you perceive the victims. It is how the perpetrator sees them. While it is difficult to imagine it, consider the fact this restaurant was outside of city limits and, as such, not a pillar of the community. If the killer had any notion she was providing drugs to this Meeks girl, it could be assumed he thought of Miss Smith as a drug dealing reprobate. It would certainly fit in with his sense of justice."

"And the laundress?"

"Well, it does present a different set of circumstances. As she was the first victim, there might have been something different to incite this killer. Her looks or perhaps she may have rejected him and then he sought what he considered easier targets. At the very least, he got his first taste of killing with her."

"Have you two ever come across any killer like that?"

"Right before the Crash of '29," Gallison chimed in, "there was a defrocked priest who killed two men who had frequented prostitutes. One guy was a banker and the other was a store owner. He said he was trying to save them from the same fate as him. The priest apparently got caught with a young female parishioner of, shall we say, dubious virtue and was kicked out of the church."

"What happened to him?" I asked.

"Never went to trial. He died insane from syphilis."

It was close to four o'clock when Eliot joined us to check up on our progress.

"Nothing new, chief, but not for trying," Gallison commented, as gracious as Santa. "The guy's got a brain in him. Could use another quality detective in our department."

I was sincerely flattered. I was just a policeman walking a beat in Ark City trying to keep a small Kansas town safe for the good people there. I no longer had any desire to be a big shot in a big city. It was a notion left me years ago as a teenager and then again somewhat more recently. But, at the very least, to be respected for my abilities gave me a renewed sense of purpose. At the moment, there was no doubt I was Baron Witherspoon and not Eric Kimble. At the moment.

"What about a libation before bed time, kids?" Eliot seemed like a college fraternity brother rather than a decorated police officer. His outgoing nature made it easier for me to relax and not be so worried. Lindsay and Gallison had just given me some worthwhile info and speculated on notions I couldn't have come up with. They were just like Sells and Rackler, homicide detectives in a big city, but with less pressure and little to gain they were able to think more creatively. I didn't really need to extend my stay much further except for the hospitality.

Flannery's Pub brought back memories of Chicago and Deanie and Bugs and Hymie and, yes, Jake Hickey. Before it soured for me, the North Side Gang tried to be like family. Hearing Dion O'Banion in my mind, the big Irish lug, sing Cohan's "Over There" and smiling like a galoot seemed like Ted Healey and his Stooges but in the end it's what saved my life.

Other than the medicinal hooch I was able to pick up every now and then, I wasn't much of a drinker. I was scared it might loosen my tongue and allow all kinds of things to slip out. Eliot Ness, on the other hand, enjoyed his whiskey shots with a beer chaser, and regaled us with stories of Prohibition-era Chicago, little realizing I personally knew many of the men he encountered. Lindsay and Gallison smiled at the hundredth retelling of the stories.

"Boss, don't you think your wife will wonder where you are?" a concerned Gallison expounded.

"No. She knows." The smile remained but it was a mask covering a deep disappointment. He snapped out of it, like a patient coming out of a coma. "The perpetrator in Wichita. He's following the case."

"How do you know?" I asked.

"If it is a person with a moral sense, an avenging angel so to speak, he doesn't want to be in the shadows. He wants to be recognized for his work. At the appropriate time, he'll reveal himself."

"Just give himself up?"

"No, no. He's going to say something or do something which might sound simple minded. But it's his way of letting you know he is doing a job, completing a task."

"Are you saying I already know the guy or have

met him?"

Ness was staring blankly ahead. I couldn't tell if he was a mystic in a trance or just another drunk expounding on his theories.

"What Eliot is indicating," Lindsay picked up, "is most of these mission oriented perpetrators let their motivation be known. They can't hide it because they want you to know they have a goal in mind. It's like our torso killer, only…"

"You don't know what the goal is." I hated having to finish his thought. We realized we were both dealing with cases unlike anything most police anywhere had ever encountered.

Chapter Twenty-Nine

My head seemed to contain a small jazz combo with the bass and drums playing most of the song. My face drooped, like it was melting away from my skull. I had stayed out too late and underestimated Eliot's ability to put away booze, never considering he had a hollow leg. Lindsay had been the first to go. Even big Detective Gallison had had enough by the fifth round. Seeing as how I relied on Eliot for transportation, I was left with him until the Mick bartender at Flannery's announced last call.

Surprisingly, Eliot was chipper and not looking the worse for wear when I got to his office the next morning. I figured it was dangerous to not be able to feel anything by drinking so much. At least I realized not to do it again.

"So, you heading home to Kansas?"

"Nothing more I can learn here, although you have opened my eyes to quite a bit."

"Well, Gallison expressed my sentiments as well. If you ever get a hankering for the city life, we'll have a place for you."

As we shook hands, Lindsay burst in without so much as a notification from Miss Hammersmith. He was as white as a sheet, a fine bead of sweat on his forehead.

"He struck again," Lindsay said bluntly.

"What?" Eliot's hand fell from mine, balling up in a fist, his knuckles practically white.

"Torso of a woman dumped at 9th and Lakeside."

"Lakeside and ninth?" Eliot's voice squeaked like a little girl. "Why, that's just…"

He turned sharply, looking out the window behind him, his hands in the same position on the window ledge. The body had been dumped within view of Eliot's office. The killer was playing a game.

Eliot turned around, straightened his vest and jacket, ran a hand over his hair to smooth down the one strand that had come loose. His voice, when he spoke, was tight but clear with a slight crack in it.

"Detective Lindsay, would you be so kind as to give Officer Witherspoon a ride to the train station?" He looked at me and finished the handshake we started. "Baron, it was a pleasure to have met you. We would relish the opportunity to work with you professionally if it were to happen."

"The honor is all mine."

I didn't look back when I left, didn't even wink at Miss Hammersmith. Lindsay's silence on the brief ride to the train station spoke more than any commentary could have. A mumbled appreciation for meeting me was more than likely due to his thoughts being elsewhere, such as a seemingly impossible case to solve and a boss who was out of sorts yet maintaining every bit of composure. For all of two days I met and worked with Eliot Ness, I could feel the knots in his stomach. I felt them myself with Natalie Dixon.

The journey back took as many stops and the same amount of time yet felt so much longer. I slept very little, recalling each and every moment of my time in

Cleveland, not just the departure, and thinking about what I learned from men who took their work seriously and too often personally. Each significant case I was involved with over the last four years was something eating at me from the inside out. This wasn't Rogelio Lopez getting drunk on a Friday night. This wasn't the kids from the high school knocking over people's mail boxes. This wasn't even the theft of eighty-two year old Edmond Hansel's bicycle. These were all cases in which I was directly involved. Wichita decided to go in another direction for their investigation. They could have learned a lot from these men.

I reported directly to Chief Richardson when I got back in about four in the afternoon. I was prepared right then and there to file a report or as he had indicated "telling him all about my vacation." He figured the traveling was pretty rough and indicated I still had another week's worth of time off. I wasn't sure I needed anything more than a long night's rest in my own bed.

Miss Banister was surprised I wasn't hungry, especially with the roast she had made and the mashed potatoes and brown gravy. Her recent new boarder, Josiah Wainwright, indicated he would have my plate so it wouldn't go to waste. He was a skinny man who worked as a laborer and could certainly use the extra meal.

I sat at the desk in my room, and made a series of notes, as much for me as for some unnecessary report. It was important to put everything in perspective and not just compare diverse cases. When it dawned on me the Wichita Police Department might never invite me back, I wondered what all this was for. I had gotten a notion in my head that I and I alone could solve this case. What I realized was it took a bunch of guys working together. And some luck.

Dave Morton dropped by toward the end of my second week, carrying with him the latest *Traveler.*

"Seems you missed all the excitement," he said smiling.

The article indicated the Cleveland Police Department, led by Public Safety Director Eliot Ness, conducted a raid in the shanty towns in and around Kingsbury Run based on a tip a possible suspect of a series of grisly murders might be there. After a thorough search, the entire area was burned down. The cause of the fires was uncertain, and there was no indication any suspect had been brought in for questioning. Eliot probably thought there could be no Mad Butcher if Kingsbury Run didn't exist. It would take some time to see if the theory worked.

After my vacation, I had an informal debriefing with Chief Richardson. He looked upon my trip like I had gone away to college and learned a few things which might be helpful for our own department over the course of time. As for Wichita's investigation, he made it very clear I was no longer involved with them if you could even say I was to begin with. The only thing I felt for certain was I had become Baron Witherspoon, beat cop in Arkansas City, Kansas; the kid who went from farm boy to war veteran to the career he had been meant to have all along. Eric Kimble wouldn't have been here; neither would the real Baron Witherspoon. I had become someone I could understand and accept without fighting off the ghosts from the past.

The summer was starting to fade and the cool breezes of fall were making their way across the plains. It was approaching Labor Day when I got a phone call from Wichita.

Chapter Thirty

Chief Richardson kept the caller waiting an inordinately long period of time, showing the same degree of respect for them as they did for me. When I got to his office, I noticed more of a smirk on his face than I had ever seen before.

"Remember, Baron, you don't owe them anything."

One thing I had learned from my trip to Cleveland was how to be and remain a professional at all times. I was forty, a veteran of the war, and a respectable police officer. If those factors alone weren't enough, I don't know what might have been.

The caller was Captain Randolph Merton. He sounded like an overly educated bureaucrat who hadn't spent a day walking a beat. He was trying to sound gracious, his words sweeter than maple syrup, but he came off as a highfalutin society mogul with an attitude about all the "little people," one of which included me. He was practically choking on his words as they came out of his mouth.

"I am calling at the behest of Chief Bowery."

"I thought Wilson was your police chief." Having a little fun making Merton squirm did not, in my mind, undermine my sense of professionalism.

"L.E. Bowery will be taking over the first of next year and was reevaluating some of our open cases."

"Like your ripper?"

"Yes. Exactly. The reports you filed indicated a direction our detectives had not previously considered."

"I got the impression they didn't want to consider it." It was necessary to make it perfectly clear to this bigwig I knew what I was doing and didn't feel his own detectives had a clue. "Detectives Sells and Rackler seem to have had their own notions."

"All of which have run their course after thorough review."

It was right there I knew I was at a fork in the road. I could have told this bloated oaf to go straight to blazes and figure out their own cases. However, it was the professional in me pulling harder. I didn't actually want to say no. I wanted to be asked back. I wanted to show them I knew how to solve a complex crime. I wanted to make amends for Natalie. Which is why I let him go on.

"With your Chief's permission, of course, we would greatly appreciate you reviewing the case files again." There was a pause, a kind of fuzzy hum in the silence. "Oh, and something else."

"Yes?"

"There's been another killing."

The bottom line is the city of Wichita had a killer running loose with his own sense of purpose, perhaps a list, certainly an agenda, and they had nothing in terms of a suspect. I had just seen the same sort of thing in Cleveland. You would like to think you can solve all these cases but you know you can't. Maybe in a smaller town, if it even happened there. But in the big cities with all the people living there and plenty of places to hide out and disappear within, there was no guarantee. Detective Sells would eventually retire. Detective

Rackler would move up in the department. Chief Wilson would spend his elder days fishing. And the Wichita Ripper would be caught or never be found. This is the way Life worked, and we didn't have much say in the matter.

Officer Ronald Roché greeted me upon my arrival. Like a younger brother or a puppy dog, his eagerness caught me off guard. He had been personable and respectful when I first met him but keeping a distance. Now, he was as happy to see me as a young kid with a sweet tooth was to see the Easter bunny.

"I didn't expect to be back here," I commented, sounding as though I had just awakened.

"Well, after I saw the news article, I knew you would be."

Officer Roché pulled a folded copy of the *Cleveland Plain Dealer* from under his arm, opened it up and smoothed it out to the article on page three. It was about a week after the burning of Kingsbury Run. Eliot Ness had caught some serious flak for it, tried to justify it as an attempt at apprehending a 'major suspect' but wound up incurring the wrath of city officials. In his desperate plea to indicate how much effort had gone into the case, he referenced the four local detectives plus having called in an 'experienced consultant, Officer Baron Witherspoon from the Arkansas City (Kansas) police department.' I knew why Ness used my name and it didn't bother me much. I wasn't anything special and I knew it. But the politicos in Cleveland didn't know it either. Now the big boys in Wichita thought I was the cat's meow. I smiled just a bit and pulled back my shoulders, feeling like the cock of the walk.

"You are somethin' after all, aren't you?" But this was not like I was the college football star who had come back to give the guys the rah-rah-pep talk. This was Death, cold and vicious death, not some misguided battle among generals, but a man, a creature of some sort, on a mission no one could possibly understand.

"Before we go in," I said, stopping in the middle of the hallway, "what do you know about the most recent victim?"

"Young girl from Oklahoma named Carole Cox. She'd been involved with Sister Celeste David."

"Who's she?"

"Sister Celeste? She has one of the biggest revivals in this area. Well, she's mostly from Texas and Oklahoma. Just making her way up to Kansas."

"And this Cox girl?"

"Apparently she'd been traveling with Sister Celeste, trying desperately to find the Lord."

I guess her search was successful after all.

I left Ronald behind as I entered the detectives' room where I first met Sells and Rackler. They were there along with Captain Merton. Rackler was looking anywhere but at me while Sells had his head buried in a file. Merton was taller than Big Ray Vernon with jet black hair and a painted on smile. He had a face like lacquer, pulled back into a clownish mask. Everything about him was fake.

"Chief Bowery and Chief Wilson are in meetings with the Commissioner at the time and send their apologies." I stood still, didn't make a sound or a move. I wanted my face and all the scars to speak for me. "These detectives have been instructed to provide their full cooperation and place all the resources of the

Wichita Police Department at your disposal."

"With all due respect, Captain, I'm just a beat cop from Ark City."

Rackler's head popped up faster than a prairie dog from a burrow.

"You see. That's what—"

"John!" Sells' voice pounded the air like shoes on pavement. The look on Rackler's face was of a bloodhound who just got swatted in the nose.

"What makes you think I've got anything to add?" I continued.

"We have seven women murdered in as many months. With all the officers and detectives assigned to this case, we haven't turned up a single viable lead. I've been instructed to find a way to bring this case to a close, and I will use any means to do so. You come highly regarded by your own chief and by Eliot Ness who is mired in a similar predicament."

"And he's no closer to solving those killings either."

"So be it. At least with you, we can say we tried."

He looked at me with an apologetic frown, the look of a tired and desperate man, not unlike Ness. As he started to leave, I said, "Captain Merton, you don't get to put this one all on my shoulders. Your men need to carry their weight."

His lips were tight and his nostrils flared slightly.

"They know that."

He left faster than Noah on his ark when the rains came. The storm was coming fast.

Chapter Thirty-One

I clapped my hands together to wake these boys up from their lackluster dreaming.

"All right. Let's get started."

For the first time in my life, I actually rolled up my sleeves. I imagine it was something Baron Witherspoon, the young farmer, would have done many times. For me, as a dapper teenage kid running with the North Side Gang, you only rolled up your sleeves to prevent blood from getting on your cuffs when you were working a guy over.

I handed them a summary of my previous analysis as well as the conclusion determined by consulting with the Cleveland detectives. Linda Kuchenberg was kind enough to type these up for me in duplicate with carbon paper. It looked professional. This was what I wanted these men to see, same as their counterparts under the jurisdiction of Eliot Ness. Perhaps they would be willing to cooperate so we could catch this beast.

Instead of looking at my face and not being able to see a person, I was trying like heck to make them realize I was a cop, same as them. As much as I disliked Rackler and started to distrust Sells, we were all in the same boat. This had to be done together.

"What you seem to have is a mission oriented perpetrator."

"A what?" There was breath and spit flying out of

Rackler's mouth. "No, what we have here is a lunatic."

"Even a lunatic has a purpose, a method to their madness."

"And just how are we supposed to figure out his method?"

"We get inside his head."

Sells had a smile on his face. He was glad to put Rackler through the wringer but also pleased to finally understand I would have made a good detective. It was he who got the ball rolling on the discussion, slowly drawing Rackler in by asking him questions and getting him to think about the answers. It was an entirely different approach for this young gung-ho bruiser of a cop who was really a detective in name only. I figured he knew and would need to crack a good case in order to be respected accordingly.

Sells, on the other hand, seemed like the guy from the Bible who was raised from the dead. When I first encountered him, he seemed old and tired. Perhaps I was concerned, maybe even fearful of winding up like him some day. Droopy eyes. Never fully shaven. Didn't seem to mind his suit wasn't pressed. Passing for a drunk in a bar rather than a Wichita police detective. This conversation put a gleam in his eye. You could see him thinking and remembering what it was like to actually care.

"So, what is his mission?" Rackler was sounding like a sweet innocent schoolboy.

"For that," I continued, "we have to see what these victims have in common to make them a target."

"A young girl who worked in a laundry. Three prostitutes. A dancer in a theater show. The owner of a slop house outside of town. And a wayward revival girl.

Doesn't seem like a whole lot of common ground, Witherspoon." I could tell Sells was starting to slip back into boredom and frustration. If it wasn't going to come easy, I might lose him.

"Think. Think of anything. Just say it out loud."

He nodded his head, willing to give it a go.

"Ok, the prostitutes are motivated by sex."

"But so was the dancer girl." Rackler was starting to play the game, too.

"Correct. However, Tangerine Smith wasn't involved with the profession. And neither was the laundry girl." I was feeling a bit like Bill Tilden, lobbing the ball back.

"But you said Tangerine Smith was giving drugs to this—" Sells reviewed the report again "—Shirley Meeks. That's moral corruption."

"Wait a minute," Rackler said, holding his hand up like a traffic cop. "The Jessica Rabal kid. Nothing to do with sex or drugs. How does she fit in?"

"She was the first," I responded as quickly as the thought came to me. "She was the one who got him started." I paused for a moment trying to get the rest of the thought from the back of my head to my tongue. When I saw Rackler starting to speak, I continued. "He knew her. He must have known her. And she rejected him somehow. After her, he knew what he had to do."

"Which was what?" Rackler's tone was almost pleading, as though he desperately wanted to know.

I was starting to see it fall into place. The mission was punishment for what the perpetrator saw as violations of morality, whether by some actual guideline or based on his own personal sense. The last killing, this Carole Cox, was a girl who had traveled with a revivalist. It seemed like a good place to start.

"What have you got on this Cox girl?" I asked no one in particular.

Rackler reached behind him for a file.

"Cox, Carole. Aged 23. Born Ponca City, Oklahoma September 4, 1915. Truancy. Runaway. Arrested for panhandling in Oklahoma City 1936. Shows up working for Sister Celeste off and on for the next year plus."

"Anything like prostitution or drugs?" It wasn't panning out. So far.

Rackler went through the file, reading it over twice while shaking his head.

"So how does she fit in?" Sells didn't sound like he was challenging but he was as eager for answers as the rest of us. I looked back at Rackler.

"What do you have on this Sister Celeste?"

He reached back again and pulled out a substantially larger file. I whistled in amazement.

"Don't get too impressed, Witherspoon. It's a lot of talk." He opened the file. "Clara Dietrich. Born Randolph, Massachusetts, July 3, 1882. Married Dr. Jordan David, thoracic surgeon at Beth Israel Hospital on March 6, 1903. The doctor was eleven years her elder. Apparently, Mrs. David was bored being a young surgeon's wife, accusations of marital infidelity led to a divorce three years later. Nothing at all for ten years until she emerged as a pacifist encouraging President Wilson to keep us out of war. Since it didn't work, she seems to have reinvented herself as Sister Celeste David and made her way to this part of the country. There have been claims of liquor sales, procurement of young women for immoral purposes, and shady financial deals. Nothing stuck. She's got a following as big as an army."

"Yeah, an army of religious crazies," Sells chimed in.

"Any one of which could be our guy." Rackler thought he was half way to solving the case.

I got an idea, went over to the office door, opened it, and called out for my liaison. Officer Roché approached cautiously, uncertain if he should enter. I waved him in.

"Ron, you had mentioned Sister Celeste before as though you were familiar with her."

"Yes. My mother and I—" He looked up and over toward Rackler and Sells. His face turned slightly red with embarrassment.

"Go on."

"Well, we've been to her revivals before. My mother actually talked with her at length last time she visited."

"About what?"

"I don't know. It was private."

"You plan on going to see her this time?"

He was looking at Rackler and Sells and not just in their direction. He stood up taller, shoulders held back, chest just a little bit pushed out. No one was going to think poorly or say anything insulting about his mother.

"Mother said she wanted to."

"Would you mind if I went along with you?"

He looked back to me like a puppy dog with wide eyes, perhaps seeing me as something a bit more than an older brother. I was showing interest in something very important to him.

"Not at all." We discussed meeting at his house

and having a light supper before the revival at the Lawrence Athletic Field. Somehow Sister Celeste could afford to rent out a baseball stadium. The plan was I would be inside the facility trying to arrange for a meeting with Sister Celeste while Rackler and Sells lurked outside, observing the people who were coming to attend, looking for anyone who had a look of suspicion. It was a long shot, to be sure. But we felt if the perpetrator was one of Sister Celeste's "army" the chances are he would be there, waiting for a sign to continue on his mission.

Chapter Thirty-Two

It would have been out of place for me to wear my uniform. It could be seen as a slap in the face to Sister Celeste and her followers as well as indicating to the perpetrator we guessed would be there. Rackler and Sells thought we did. Even I gave in to the excitement of a possibility. Given the fact there hadn't been even a lead, our feelings were understandable. It was a step in the right direction.

I couldn't recall the last time I wore a suit. It dawned on me it was at Beth Handy's wedding. From her nuptials to tracking down a killer at a revival meeting. I was going to have to either hang up the suit for good or get out to more places.

I was instructed to come for supper at five o'clock. It was to be a light meal so as to not become overly full for the passion of the meeting. The indication was Sister Celeste delivered intense sermons which instilled an energy and vibrancy, some said, delivered by God himself. I knew people of the sort but they were mostly drunks. Perhaps some of the faithful were drunk on something divine.

Deanna Roché was dressed in a white cloth gown with lace trim everywhere. Her hair was pulled back in a large soft bun with just two wispy strands lazily drooping and landing softly on her neck. Her red lipstick made her skin seem whiter than it was. Yet, there didn't appear to be anything pure about her, especially how her gaze captured my eyes, almost wanting to get inside of me. It was unnerving in a way I hadn't experienced before. Even facing down a beast like Carson Stankey didn't make me as uncomfortable as looking at her.

"I am so glad to see you again, Baron." Apparently, our prior meeting was enough for her to dismiss formalities. "I am even more pleased you will be joining us this evening. Sister Celeste has a way, oh, how shall I say it, a way of helping you redefine your life." I wondered how her life had been redefined.

"Perhaps I'm ready."

Cold sliced meat, potato salad, and lemonade made the evening meal feel more like a picnic. However, with everything being served on fine China and the beverages in crystal glasses, Deanna Roché was creating an elegant setting. I knew she didn't have many opportunities to do so, certainly not with a shy son who was a police officer. Perhaps this is how she wanted her life to be or maybe she was trying to make me believe this is how it always was. For the moment, I was just another performer in her play.

Ronnie drove us in his mother's car, a Cadillac Coupé, probably four or five years old. It was a dark gray, not quite silver, with a deep maroon leather interior. The car was polished to a mirror-like shine, and it was doubtful if it was used much. Ronnie drove while we sat in the crowded back seat. It felt like some weird Hollywood-style limousine with a chauffeur, the three of us going to a meeting to celebrate the kind of riches money can't buy. Or maybe a major studio movie premiere.

I caught sight of Sells as we entered, assumed Rackler was somewhere on the opposite side, hopefully paying careful attention to the crowd that was entering the stadium. A tall slender man, balding with sunken eyes, wearing a black suit with a red bow tie, walked toward Deanna. She smiled in recognition as he approached. He held out his arm for her and escorted us to a covered section with better seats. He left us without once saying a word. Whatever passed between them was simply understood.

"Sister Celeste knew we'd be here." Deanna Roché was proud of her acquaintance with a woman who could save her soul. From what, I wasn't sure.

At precisely eight o'clock, the lights within the stadium turned off suddenly. There was a collective gasp followed by a buzzing like bees ready to swarm and then a few quieting the others down until a loud "SSSHHH" fell like snowflakes and covered everything. Just as suddenly, spotlights were turned on to a stage in the middle of the stadium. It was perhaps ten feet high and most likely had steps in back. The figure on the stage was dressed in a pure white gown with a garland of flowers in her hair. Her head was lifted to the heavens and her arms raised, reaching for the inspiration. She finally lowered her head and spoke.

"First Timothy. Chapter five. Verse twenty. 'Them that sin reprove before all: that the rest also may have fear.' This is how we face evil in our times, my friends. This is how we win the battle. If the archangel Michael can fight Satan over the body of Moses, what kind of effort can we make in the war against wickedness, vice, and immorality? We can do no less, my friends. No less. We must be vigilant. We must be strong. We must have complete faith in the Lord."

It was exactly this kind of preaching which would arouse someone to take action, make someone believe not enough was being done for the sake of righteousness, convincing them they alone could rid the world of sin. I felt sure the perpetrator was in the stadium right then and there. But as we had gathered from our interviews, he remained in the shadows.

Because of where we sat, we had to look up at the stage. I saw Deanna's eyes reflecting the bright lights, embracing them, bathing in the glow of what she surely must have felt was a divine blessing. Ronnie didn't have any particular look on his face, just blank, but he nodded in agreement. It wasn't easy to tell if he was as passionate about Sister Celeste as his mother or if he was going along for the ride.

"She's got an interesting background," I practically whispered leaning over to him.

"I know. I read the file on Rackler's desk."

I wasn't sure at what surprised me more: he was aware of who Sister Celeste really was or he had the nerve to look at the file and risk Rackler's anger.

It was well over an hour of Biblical quotations, passionate encouragement, call-and-response, recorded music played over the loudspeakers which usually announced the next batter, and subtle references regarding donations. These, naturally, would lead to promises fulfilled. At the end, the lights went out on the stage and then came up slowly on the stadium. Sister Celeste and her group were nowhere to be found. It was then the tall slender man in the black suit came over to us.

"Sister Celeste requests your presence for an

audience." He extended his arm in general. With my hand on her shoulder, I guided Deanna toward him. She took his hand and started walking away but he stood there looking at Ronnie and me. "She would like to meet with all of you." This was an opportunity too good to pass up.

Chapter Thirty-Three

It was a small room perhaps used for meetings or offices but in this case a waiting area for the faithful. In this case, Deanna Roché and perhaps her son Ronnie. I hadn't figured out yet how devoted he was to the Lord or to his mother. He appeared to show a degree of embarrassment when he admitted in front of Rackler and Sells he would be attending this event. I always felt as though he stuck close to his mother because neither of them had any one else. It was something I could easily relate to.

The silence was almost frightening. It was as though Deanna was expecting the Rapture and Ronnie was witnessing the Crucifixion. I was simply hoping to find a killer. And here we all were together.

The young girl who entered had hair the color of pale rust, a red bordering on blonde. Her robe was as white as Sister Celeste's but it was made out of cotton without any of the fine lace attached to it. Her smile was as wide as the morning sunrise and as bright.

"How good of you to come. Sister Celeste appreciates you are willing to have an audience with her." She walked directly over to Deanna, holding her by the shoulders, ready to embrace her as a supplicant. "I don't know if you remember me. I'm Katie Moore, Sister Celeste's personal assistant. I was here for your meeting with her."

"Yes. Yes." Deanna may or may not have recalled young Miss Moore but she was not saying at this time. She recollected her profound discussion and the life-changing words she had heard. This was only a guess on my part. I didn't cotton much to these types of religious zealots, certainly not after all the death and destruction and chaos I had personally encountered in my life. It worked for some and that was all right. At this time, however, we were looking for a monster among the angels.

Whatever bright light came from the smile of Katie Moore was dimmed, a gray cloud compared to the ultimate brightness represented by Sister Celeste David. She burst into the room like a shooting star and all worldly notions vanished. She made them diminish so the only thoughts you would have were of her and her alone. Some peddlers sold ointments and cure-alls, bottles filled with alcohol and herbs and strange ingredients. Sister Celeste sold something even more desperate: hope.

She beheld the awe in Ronnie's eyes and recognized the devotion of Deanna. But it was me she fixed upon and walked over to as though I had the Holy Grail in my back pocket. Her hands extended and almost pleading, her fingers touched my face and traced the lines of my scars. It was nothing like Dr. Brenz had ever done. It was something closer to a lover's touch. In this regard, she had more in common with Deanna.

"I am honored to have you here, Officer Witherspoon. Your presence fills us with admiration." I didn't recall ever introducing or announcing myself in any fashion. It scared me to think how completely in control she was. It also made me wonder how much she knew. "Mrs. Roché and her son think very highly of you."

"It is I who am honored." I figured I would try playing her game even though I pretty much guessed she had me figured out. I couldn't match her vocabulary but at this point there was nothing really to lose.

"You have seen Hell, looked into the eyes of Satan, and returned to fight on the side of the Lord. There is nothing you should fear."

"Except the unknown."

"Everything is known unto the Lord. Put your faith in him."

I smiled at her, not for any reason I could figure and perhaps only to buy me the time to think of a response. She apparently knew much about me once, I assume, Deanna Roché told her I would be coming. She must have had a complete collection of agents who could find out all manner of information. This was part of her organization. This was what made her unique and special to her adherents and gave her sway over their opinions. But I knew she didn't know everything about me. I had the feeling of still being in control.

"Until the Lord guides me to the killer of these women, I will trust in my own instincts." I made sure my tone sounded challenging and defiant to let her know I did not accept her gospel nor her guidance. I didn't have to worry Deanna or Ronnie were going to be offended because they knew I was not a believer.

"They will only take you so far, Baron. The righteous have secrets that will set you upon the right path."

She placed her hands firmly on either side of my head, looked up toward the sky, brought my head down, kissed my forehead firmly, and then lifted my head and kissed me firmly on the lips. Her hands disengaged from my head. She turned and walked out of the room, followed devotionally by Katie Moore who appeared slightly jealous at not being able to offer the same blessing. The sun had set and it was now dark as night. The blessings of Sister Celeste gone, we were once again on our own.

It appeared as though Deanna and Ronnie Roché were slighted as Sister Celeste had said nothing to them. As it was not my intention to take attention away from the truly devoted, it felt awkward in the silence of the room. I knew I had nothing to say. I was not there for any one else's uplifting. There was a murder investigation in progress. I walked out of the room and hoped they would follow.

The late summer air was humid making me sticky and wet. I was covered in sweat from just standing outside. However, I couldn't be sure if it wasn't the strange embrace and kiss by Sister Celeste making me feel put off. An awkward lump stuck in my throat. I needed a glass of cold water or a whiskey.

This time, I sat up front with Ronnie while his mother sat alone in the back seat. It was my hope I could get him to open up and tell me more about Sister Celeste I didn't already know.

"Her real name is Clara Dietrich. There have been some accusations made about her." I spoke now as a policeman, trying to shake him out of his dream-like state.

"I know. I've known about her for a while. I go for my mother. You understand, don't you?" There was almost a pleading tone to his voice as though he were expecting me to forgive him. I didn't know what there was to forgive.

When we got back to the house, I stepped out first, came around to the driver's side, and opened the door for Deanna. My outstretched hand was a way to show her the respect I felt she did not get from the one place she expected to get it.

"I am honored you joined us at this solemn event," she said softly, almost whispering. Suddenly, she placed her hands on either side of my head, pulled it down to kiss my forehead, then lifted my head to kiss me on the lips, exactly as Sister Celeste had done. She turned gracefully and walked toward the front door. Ronnie looked like he had just swallowed a bug and followed her. I didn't mean to be in a position to cause any rift especially since I still needed his help. But I did wonder if Deanna Roché was trying to mimic Sister Celeste or if she had other ideas.

Chapter Thirty-Four

I got to the detectives' room what I thought was rather early but was extraordinarily surprised to see Detective Rackler sitting at his desk, sleeves rolled up, and wearing eyeglasses. He took them off immediately upon seeing me. It would have been too easy to make a smart aleck comment. I saved those for when they counted.

Sells came in a moment later carrying a big stack of files. He put half of them on Rackler's desk and sat down at his with the rest.

"Anything from last night?" I asked.

"We recognized a guy going in, name of Eli Railsback. Claims he's an anarchist even though the anarchists will have nothing to do with him." Sells was shaking his head in apparent disgust. "When he came out, he was a little agitated."

"Agitated? Agitated how?"

"Punching his fist into his hand. Mumbling to himself. We followed him to a bar in Delano. He got drunk and left. Talked to the bartender who told us he gets drunk a lot. He's got no record to speak of. If he is an anarchist, he's an awfully bad one."

"What are all these?" my head nodding toward the stack of files.

"Every stabbing death in Wichita in the last twenty years. Figured maybe we could find a pattern."

"No." Rackler's comment was expelled with a frustrated gasp. "I have learned one thing."

"Oh?"

"It's amazing how many ways you can get stabbed."

I understood their frustration, the same as I saw in Cleveland. Those tasked to protect the public feeling themselves handcuffed. Unable to do their jobs due to pressure beyond their control. However, this was the only way to get it done, keep reviewing every case, every file, every incident, think beyond what you knew even as bizarre as it might sound. This perpetrator was only logical within his own mind. It would take a great deal for any one of us to think in the same manner.

"We're missing something." I blurted it out without thinking about.

"You're damned right we are." I tried picturing Rackler saying that with his glasses to prevent me from starting an argument.

"I'm going back and talking with those witnesses again."

"Who? The pimp and the madam?"

"And the rest."

"You want me to go with you?" I wasn't sure if Sells' interest in joining me was to see what I was thinking about, to avoid the endless files, or to get away from Rackler for a day or two.

"No. I'm changing out of my uniform and just going as a citizen. I think someone knows something and just doesn't feel right saying it."

I saw Officer Roché round the corner and head toward the detectives' room as I left. I just wasn't ready to face him and discuss his mother. I also needed to be able to speak to some of these folks as confidentially as possible. Ronnie Roché came across as awkward even though he was well meaning. At this point in the investigation, I needed to be on my own.

The young black maid at Miss Becky's house indicated she was not yet awake. I moved on to the theater and tracked down Melinda Malone. She said it was okay to talk with her as long as I was able to follow and keep up with her.

"Life in the theater moves fast, Officer Witherspoon. We need to keep up with it."

"Were there any strange men who approached Ms. Delsin, either before, during, or after any shows?"

"Strange men and pretty dancers go hand in hand. In her case she attracted men about your age, more than likely married, but with enough charm to convince her they could offer her the moon."

"Any one in particular stand out?"

"They all seemed the same to me."

Malone saw all young women as sex-starved kittens and all men as Lotharios. It was as though all of her life was a theater.

Shep Breckman was in his dressing room gargling with something smelling of pine tar. He held up a finger to advise me to wait as he finished his last spit.

"Got to keep the pipes loose. Old timer from back in the day recommended it. It's a combination of..."

"It's quite all right." Knowing what it was would probably have made me sicker than watching him gargle with it. "I'm trying to determine if Valeria had any regular visitors."

"Visitors? Great word. I like that. No, more like customers, officer. The girl had long since given up the notion of success and was looking for, what's the expression, a sugar daddy?" I nodded and started to walk off. "Wait. There was this one guy. Never did anything more than stand in the shadows in the alley behind the theater. I think she was talking to him one night when I came out. Then I heard him run off."

Miss Becky was awake by noon and graciously granted me an audience while she drank her coffee from a China cup and had her three-minute soft boiled eggs and toast. Her morning gown was still elegant with pearls sewn into the fabric and she herself made up for the evening despite the fact it was still daylight.

"I know I asked you about the night Angela and Aurora were killed. What I'd like to know is if either one of them might have had a regular client. Someone lacking confidence and only comfortable around them. Someone who may have tried to protect them or, better yet, save them."

"Officer Witherspoon, just between you and I, the pastor at the First United Methodist Church is a frequent guest. He hardly believes there is a need to save my girls."

"This may be so, Miss Becky. But there might have been someone who didn't have the pastor's perspective, shall we say."

Miss Becky sipped her coffee, bit into her toast with her front teeth like a bunny rabbit and wiped her lips with her cloth napkin.

"Angela did have a young man escort her home from time to time. He would be waiting for her at the corner as she left for the night."

"Did you ever see his face?"

"No. He always stood in the shadows."

I managed to locate Tangerine Smith's old cook, Shaughnessy Burkett, working in a slop house run by one of the churches. They catered to the homeless and poor. Burkett was a rung or two up from those he was helping so he fit right in.

"Shirley Meeks said she remembered Tangerine shooing someone off right before she was killed. You know who it might have been?"

"No, sir. Miss Tangerine took in all kinds, like some people take in stray dogs."

"You remember anyone in particular?"

"I seen her talking to someone one night, out back of the restaurant. Short feller. He been standing in the shadows."

When I went back to Delano, I simply stood in the door, not moving, basically blocking it, the same way Montisse blocked the passage to the back room. This time, without my uniform, I didn't appear official. It didn't mean I was going to be intimidated. This punk never ran with the North Side Gang, never knew he wasn't going to push me around.

How Carson Stankey knew to come out from the back was a mystery to me. He walked slowly up to me and stood less than a foot away. Those black eyes looked dead. Suddenly, a slight smile appeared. This surprised me. He nodded for me to follow.

One small table. Two chairs. Two glasses. A bottle of brown amber liquid. The cork had been previously removed. We sat opposite each other.

"Have a drink?"

"I'd like a new bottle."

He laughed, heartily and loud.

"Do you think I would poison a cop?"

"Without a second thought."

He laughed again. Then the laughter stopped.

"You don't need a drink."

"No."

He leaned in toward me. I leaned toward him.

"What do you want?"

"To find Chantelle's killer."

"Why?"

"Because it disturbs my sense of balance."

He leaned back. I continued leaning forward.

"Balance?"

"You have your business. It's not for everyone but it's here. They make a law to get rid of you, so be it. But killing your girls is not the way to make this business go away. Someone is doing this and it is unsafe for everyone. Even those who are not associated with your business."

"I have been making inquiries."

"You wouldn't know where to begin." His eyes widened. I pushed him and needed to know when to stop before Montisse did what he did best. "You're asking other pimps and prostitutes and grifters. That's not who did this."

"Who did?"

I finally leaned back. He respected me now, understood I was better suited to this. I could stop pushing.

"The man I'm looking for stands in the shadows and doesn't want to be seen except by the girls. He wants them to notice him but no one else. He's gentle. He wants to protect the girls, maybe even save them. He'd rather be their friend than their client."

"Chantelle would take homeless men to a diner and

get them fed. She would do such things. Is this someone who would kill her?"

"Perhaps. Did you see her with anyone…special?"

He shook his head. He may have been looking at me but he was in deep thought trying to remember all the men Chantelle had ever slept with. It wasn't going to be determined in an hour or even a day. At least, I had gotten him to consider what I was looking for. I stood up and nodded at him, then started to leave.

"If I think of anything, I will send for you."

I kept walking, my back to him as a sign of trust. There were still no answers. Only a figure in the shadows.

Chapter Thirty-Five

It was Friday morning. I was tired. I hadn't slept much. It was barely a week since I returned to Wichita. I learned a few things but nothing useful enough to catch this killer. It dawned on me I was putting in the majority of the effort for something that was completely out of my jurisdiction. There was no desire to be Eliot Ness or J. Edgar Hoover. I was a small-town cop and I liked it that way in spite of the thrill and excitement of the investigation.

What a funny thought! *I was a small-town cop and I liked it that way.* I had become a cop in Ark City, Kansas having originally been a student of gangsters. I had been on the path to silk suits and fast cars and women who wanted me because I could treat them well. When Dion O'Banion suggested I go off to war, he would never have imagined I would eventually become a beat cop in a small Kansas burg or be respected by the man who was credited for sending Capone away. There was no telling where the road would lead now.

I had no idea how long Rackler and Sells had been in the office. But at eight a.m. it appeared they had been there overnight. Rackler's hair looked as though it had been combed by a tractor. Sells swilled his coffee. When they finally realized I was there, they looked up to see an unlikely smile on my face.

"The look of police work." I had no intention of

insulting them but this was the first time they looked bothered by this case beyond the pressure they were getting from the big wigs. This was the way I must have looked trying to figure out who butchered three men in Ark City. This was the way cops were supposed to look.

"Grab a seat. We've got more files." Sells was only too happy to share the misery. However, I nodded my head negatively.

"Heading back."

"Why?"

"I've got my own job to do." As much as I relished the challenge, a sense of responsibility crept up on me like a cat in a mist.

"This thing's not solved." Rackler sounded like a little boy who was told he had to get out of the mud and take a bath.

"It's funny how it wasn't too long ago you pretty much told me you could get this thing wrapped up yourself." Rackler stared at me blankly, blinked his eyes, and looked like he might start bawling. "We've made progress but I didn't sign on for the long haul."

"You're right," Sells said as he stood up, moving slowly over to me on tired old legs. Sells leaned over more, as though there was a heavy burden on his back. He had dark circles under his eyes and a more wrinkled face. This was exactly the kind of case to do that to you. He put his hand out, and I took it. There was a nod of his head, the slightest acknowledgement of his appreciation. I turned and left.

I lost track of time. Maybe I drove slower on purpose to give myself a chance to think. It was just as likely I was trying to clear my head, knowing I had pushed myself further than ever before. Such an effort wasn't necessary in Ark City. There still may have been some political corruption but it was doubtful with Hallett no longer being a councilman. Gangsters were no longer a factor except for the few families in the county with their secret stills but they weren't hurting anyone. If the Mob was any kind of influence, you wouldn't know it. They were more organized than U.S. Steel. Being a beat cop meant keeping the peace for the benefit of the people of our community. I didn't want it any other way.

Unfortunately, I kept having visions of a man in the shadows, lurking, watching, waiting. Not very tall. Not very imposing. Almost forgettable. Quiet for the most part. Focused on the mission set in his mind. Someone you would not recognize as having these thoughts or intentions largely because he wasn't evil, only obsessed.

It dawned on me many of the notions of this possible character could have been used to describe me as well.

I got back in the late morning and went directly to Chief Richardson's office. I went over in detail everything that transpired and what we determined, even though we were no closer to an actual suspect. He agreed I had given the Wichita Police Department an adequate assessment and it was time for my return. I left the receipts for my stay on his desk for reimbursement.

It was a mistake not to get breakfast before leaving Wichita. My stomach was growling like the cowardly lion in the Oz book. There was only one cure: Daisy Mae's. A seat at the counter beckoned, and Dixie strode up to me like a schoolteacher waiting for me to blurt out my assignment.

"Meatloaf. Mashed potatoes and gravy. Side of green beans."

"I thought you didn't like meatloaf."

"When did I say that?" Her smile made me aware I passed the test.

I was sopping up the last bit of gravy when Larry Hammer came in and sat next to me. Dixie had a cup of coffee on the counter in front of him before his back side hit the seat. He's what you might call the King of Regulars. He indicated he had retired but was still doing odd jobs for Shell on account of the fact no one could do what he could. There wasn't a machine he couldn't work or fix. He figured retiring simply meant he wouldn't have to wake up as early anymore. Since he knew everyone in town for as far back forty years, Larry was the one I turned to often for the whos and hows and whys.

"Where you been?" he asked.

"Wichita."

"Thinkin' of moving?"

"Heck, no! I'm a darn sight happy to be back. Nothing up there for me except a madman. And I figure the police up there can catch him for themselves."

"Then why were you up there?"

I had to admit he had a point. A bigger city. More police. More detectives. They had everything going for them we didn't have. If anything remotely like those crimes happened here, people would be moving out of town like it had the plague. It really didn't make any sense Wichita couldn't get their man.

Then I remembered all the efforts of the officers,

detectives, and Department of Public Safety of Cleveland. They had considerably more resources, more manpower, and they were staring at a stone wall when it came to locating a monster. Whatever abilities I had or whatever abilities someone else thought I had, I was only one man. I shook the tree but no fruit came falling down. Maybe, if anything, I gave them a new way of looking at this thing.

"Damned if I know, Larry."

All I knew was I had to stop thinking about the man in the shadows. He was starting to remind me of the man in the mirror.

Chapter Thirty-Six

When I wasn't arresting drunks, tracking down lost dogs, or breaking up marital fights, I basically floated through life. There was nothing to ground me to any kind of reality. Or maybe it was any other kind of reality. This had been my world since getting back from the war, a face filled with scars and a head clouded by uncertainty. It was driving headlong into a storm to become Baron Witherspoon and become accepted on the Ark City police force, and with Dr. Brenz to keep me upright and mobile, I turned into something worthwhile. It was a responsibility I freely accepted, even though it contained no excitement.

There had been occasional pain in my face and periodic feelings like it was melting right off my skull. Doctie figured it was the techniques they used back in '18, indicated they were doing much better work now, and I would have to just deal with it if I didn't want to go someplace like Chicago or Philadelphia for more surgery. There was nothing thrilling about the prospect; by the same token, I had these dreams someone was slowly pulling a mask off my face. If it were to happen, what would they really see?

I would finally be able to go to Arkalalah, the city's official fall festival the following week in late October. I was usually stuck on duty or doing something else while the rest of the guys were enjoying the festivities. This was to be the tenth anniversary, and the Chamber of Commerce was going all out for it. Kathryn Curfman was this year's Queen Alalah. She had short hair pulled back to reveal a regal forehead and an endearing smile both uplifting as well as engaging. It's the way the Chamber of Commerce liked their queens to be.

Like Heather Devore and Jake Hickey and Natalie Dixon, the killer in the shadows in Wichita started to fade from my mind and with it any desire to be caught up in the workings of the big city. As a matter of fact, most of my desires and interests were starting to fade. At forty, I felt old, perhaps older than I was. An elderly man with false teeth and no hair and a cane to get around. I wasn't a member of a gang wearing silk suits, nor dead because of it. Twenty years later, I didn't feel much like a war hero. I missed a chance to save two women. The only thing keeping me going was stalking my prey like a hunter. I was good at it for whatever reason but now my chance was gone.

The briefest of thoughts entered my mind about transferring to the Wichita Police Department or taking Gallison and Lindsay up on their offer to work in Cleveland. But after ten or fifteen years, I would be in the same spot with no real purpose in life and no one to share my few joys and many fears.

The winter didn't give us a lot of snow but it was cold. The wind would cut through any clothes you were wearing making you feel naked and dead. My feet were stone blocks and my face was numb quite a bit of the time. The drunks stayed inside and so did the dogs. It was the kind of quiet farmers sensed before a tornado passed through. There was nothing for me to do but wake up every morning and go to sleep every night.

It was the first day of spring in 1939 Linda Kuchenberg advised me I had a call from Captain Randolph Merton of the Wichita Police Department.

"Officer Witherspoon, we've had another murder by the same killer."

"Rather unfortunate, huh?"

"Chief Richardson agreed with my assessment your prior evaluation was vital in our investigation."

"Which is in the hands of Detective Sells and Detective Rackler."

There was a pause. His tone was straightforward and direct. It also sounded like he was trying mighty hard to be courteous perhaps because he wasn't used to it.

"Detective Sells has…retired. Detective Rackler personally requested your further assistance. You have been temporarily reassigned to the Wichita Police Department's Detectives Bureau. Your living expenses and accommodations will be provided by our department. How soon can you be here?"

My first reaction was anger and a feeling I was some kind of slave or piece of property to be bought and sold. My footsteps fell hard moving down the corridor to the chief's office but I didn't blow in like one of those tornadoes.

"It's political, Baron." It was so little to say but it meant so much. "Mayor Corn, City Manager Wells, and Chief Bowery visited our City Council."

"When?"

"Last week."

"Why wasn't I told about it?"

"You're being told now."

I stared at him. I didn't mean to be disrespectful. Then it dawned on me this was what I wanted. To once again face the demon and force him back into the darkness. Or perhaps to bring a monster into the light? This time I packed a bigger bag. I left it in the car while I went to the main detectives' office. Rackler's hair was combed better than the last time I saw him. He stood up quickly and was right in front of me with his hand out in no time.

"Glad you're here."

"What happened?"

"The case went as cold as Christmas morning. There were no further killings and the pimp down in Delano and the Madame weren't as helpful with us. Sells was feeling poorly, went to the doctor right before New Year's Eve and was told he better quit before he popped a gasket. So then it was only me. And then this."

He showed me a picture of the latest victim, Marie Whitaker, another one of Carson Stankey's girls. I guess she must have been a pretty girl. Photos of the dead don't give you much. Perhaps she had a vivacious smile at one time but it was now gone forever. All I could see was a silk dress, a white lace blouse, bright red lipstick, and the knife wounds. They seemed similar to the previous victims but with more passion and aggressiveness. There was no telling why he had not continued killing as regularly as before. But one thing was for certain: he was back and he was angrier. He would either be more dangerous or, and this was the only hope we had, more prone to making a mistake.

Chapter Thirty-Seven

There had been interviews and follow-up interviews and staring at photos and autopsy reports. There were phone calls to Cleveland but only with Lindsay and Gallison as Eliot Ness was no longer in a position to comment, having burned down Kingsbury Run and getting in a heap of trouble for it. I called Sandy Clevenger at the *Traveler* because I trusted her research abilities more than anyone else's but she didn't have access to anything other than our newspaper and the material was limited. I was beginning to feel like Sells and hoped my health wasn't going to suffer for it.

Right at the end of my first week there, I ran into Ronnie Roché. There was a noticeable gasp when he saw me, not necessarily pleased but more surprised. He stood in front of me without saying a word.

"Hello, Officer Roché."

"Officer Witherspoon. I didn't know you had come back."

"Temporarily reassigned."

"On account of Sells?"

"On account of someone butchering women. Well, maybe the third time's a charm."

"Like the Trinity." He looked away for a moment, lost in thought, before turning back to me. "Mother...My mother would like to have you over for dinner." It was a surprising comment considering he

193

was just aware of my return then. "She indicated if you were ever back in town to please invite you."

"It will be a pleasure. Will tonight do?"

"Yes." He smiled and continued down the corridor. He had the disquieting appearance and attitude of a small puppy dog, and I wondered if he would ever amount to anything as a cop. He seemed efficient and professional but I guessed it was more about his upbringing from everything I had previously seen. Even a bulldog like Rackler had the moxie to say what was on his mind and go after something even if he was wrong. Ronnie was content to follow.

It was my intention to revisit all the witnesses as I read my notes over again for the hundredth time. I felt like there was something in there, beyond a figure in the shadows. However, it was frustrating to keep going back to them knowing they couldn't, or perhaps wouldn't say anything more or different. I realized it was because they were comfortable. They were in their own house, so to speak. I had to make them feel as though something were at stake. For Carson Stankey, his business could be in jeopardy. I told Rackler to bring him in to the station.

"On what charge?"

"Make something up. Jaywalking. Spitting on the sidewalk. I don't care. But we need him down here and without that brute Montisse backing him up."

Rackler brought Carson Stankey in, shoving him forward roughly by the forearm, practically forcing him into the chair like he was stuffing an extra pair of pants into a suitcase. Stankey offered minimal resistance. His facial muscles were tenser than mine could ever be and his eyes were focused like the sights on an Enfield rifle.

He was smart enough to not add any real charges to the excuse for which he had been brought in.

The room was a grayish green. One door. One rectangular wooden table. Two wooden chairs. No windows. No phone or papers or files. Just a room. There was nothing to distract your mind which meant you had to focus. You couldn't make up a story using details from the room for your imagination. You could only respond.

"All right. Stop," I said and stared at Rackler. He left the room as my gaze followed him out. I turned my attention to the tall man sitting quietly before me.

"You arresting me?"

"I don't see any handcuffs. This look like a cell to you?" My face ached. Each scar felt as though a small worm underneath the skin tried to push its way out. It wouldn't have surprised me if I was twitching. "First Chantelle and then Marie. You don't seem to be able to take care of your ladies."

A momentary burst of anger zipped through his body like a lightning bolt, eyes widened then recessed, right hand clutching the lip of the table, turning red. This was what I needed, for him to be uncomfortable enough to make it worthwhile to work with me.

"I take care of them just fine."

"The man in the shadows play any part in this?"

"Don't know. Marie was killed at home after she was done working."

"Tell me about her home."

He made his face a stone block trying to keep in control, acting like it was the private club in Delano. His features finally softened after a bit, probably because he realized I could keep him there all day, maybe all night, and without having any control it was going to take a lot more effort to remain a block of stone.

"A flop."

"You own it?"

"How did you know?"

"I guessed. Go on."

He breathed in deeply, licked his lips, and exhaled like he was in a confessional at church.

"Got a lady runs it. Bunch of rooms, maybe fifteen. One kitchen, one bathroom. They don't do business there. No men allowed. Sleep, eat, use the john. That's it."

"So, are you telling me one of the girls cut her like that?"

He leaned forward harshly, held back by imaginary shackles.

"I ain't telling you nothing."

"And if you keep telling me nothing, seems like more of your girls are going to get cut up. Less inventory. Business closes. You know there's a Depression going on, right? You might wind up selling apples on the corner of Douglas and Main."

He leaned back and started rubbing his forehead like he had a headache. I honestly didn't know what this pimp was going to be able to tell me but I had to find out everything he knew or remembered, even if it was just a small kernel of something.

"The other girls are telling me there's a guy, more like a boy, been hanging around outside the building. A couple of them say they seen him when they was out and about."

"Why do you say he was more like a boy?"

"Short, thin, almost like there was nothing to him." He was running on his own train of thought. I could see his eyes light up, not with anger. It was more like he was finally starting to put something together. Then he threw his hands in the air. "Nah, couldn't be him. A pipsqueak. He couldn't be doing this."

"Why not? Someone slight and gentle and boyish. The girls might consider him cute, certainly not threatening, allow him to get close. The cuts are deep, true, but wouldn't require a great deal of strength, especially since the girls are surprised. They let their guard down and he walked right up to them. This boy as you call him."

I don't know why I said all of it. I should have simply been thinking and contemplating for myself. At this point, however, it was necessary to talk with someone who was more familiar with the darker side of street life, the world all respectable people never wind up seeing. I knew all about it as a kid but as time passed I had developed a respectability which brought me farther away from the life of callous brutality. It was something Jake Hickey reminded me of from many years ago.

"You need to have Montisse follow the girls around at night," I continued, "see if he can't spot this guy, get a description of him, maybe even identify him."

"What you really mean is you need me to have Montisse out there doing your job. Isn't that right, cop?"

Carson Stankey was the type of guy who needed to be in control, even if it was simply the appearance of it. However, I needed to be the one pulling the strings.

This was a police investigation into multiple murders carried out over a period of time, just like the Torso Killer in Cleveland. We, the police, needed to be in control, and not let the criminal element take care of this for themselves. Citizens needed to know their cities were safe. The notion this man thought he could pull my strings after all I had been through made me angry.

I could feel the twitching. Those worms under my skin and the scars pulsed. I leaned in closely, my face inches from him.

"You're going to cooperate, Stankey. You're going to do exactly what I tell you. Otherwise, I will make it my life's mission to find a way to lock you up in a cold dark cell for the rest of your miserable life. You're an ant. You're nothing to me. And I will squash you and think nothing of it."

He finally realized I was nothing like Sells, a tired and weary veteran, or Rackler, for all his bravado. I was the same monster that had been butchering women in Wichita. It was a shock to think I could feel the same way. Maybe now I could understand him better. First, I would have to find him.

Chapter Thirty-Eight

When I was told I had been "temporarily reassigned," I knew it meant a long-term stay. I wound up packing more than a satchel for a few days. Truth be told, I had never been anywhere long enough that required more than a uniform and a fresh pair of socks. I was actually hard pressed to find a couple of clean shirts and pants appropriate enough for church, assuming I was the kind who went to church.

A dress uniform certainly wasn't ideal for my second formal dinner at the Roché residence, even though I was a policeman the same as Ronnie. I felt for some reason Deanna deserved a well dressed and respectful house guest. I certainly wasn't prepared for how the evening would turn out.

Ronnie greeted me at the door, somewhat like a servant or dutiful butler. As we were both wearing dress clothing, neither one of us resembled policemen in any fashion. He responded to me courteously but as though he had never met me before. I was escorted directly into the dining room, where Deanna stood in an elegant green velvet gown in a shade of dark moss with a deep cut revealing a healthy cleavage. It was formal yet inviting at the same time. I couldn't figure out, however, what the invitation was for.

I approached gallantly, kissed the hand she held before me, acting like one of King Arthur's knights. I was lost in a different world. It wasn't the bad boy from Chicago living the life of a Kansas farm kid. It was misty and covered in fog, dreamlike, even though I knew I wasn't sleeping.

The meal was more sumptuous than the first time. A roast with various herbs. Honey and gingered carrots. Whipped potatoes with butter. And, surprisingly, wine. Only two glasses. Near her plate and mine.

The dinner conversation was limited to the weather, the differences between Wichita and Arkansas City, and the power of prayer as exemplified by Sister Celeste. Eventually, the evening at the revival became the primary focus of the discussion. While she was pleased Sister Celeste had taken to me so deeply, I sensed a kind of envy as though Deanna was not as important.

"She was certainly gracious," I said, "but it's not the kind of thing I typically embrace." I had hoped to restore her goodwill with the charlatan preacher as I had no need of any blessings from Sister Celeste or any of her ilk.

"But you should. Her guidance is wise and powerful."

"And the righteous have secrets that will set me upon the right path?" Remembering Sister Celeste's comments, Deanna raised her glass in a toast. Her smile was just the slightest bit wicked, as though the serpent had taught her well.

Ronnie dutifully removed the dishes, passing through the swinging door separating dining room from kitchen. There was a silence beyond, not even the subtle clinking of plates or cutlery. His job was more than removing plates from the table but clearing the sounds from the room as well. Deanna walked elegantly toward the parlor and I followed. She looked back toward the kitchen, toward Ronnie, and closed the pocket doors behind us.

"Would you care for a sherry, Baron?"

"I was under the impression you didn't drink."

"Only on special occasions."

"I am grateful for the compliment but I don't feel deserving."

From a crystal decanter, she poured two drinks into small crystal glasses made for sipping. She reached out her arm, like a lioness stretching her paw, and offered me one of the glasses, and then sat on the small settee which could barely accommodate both of us. By virtue of its size, our thighs were close together. I turned toward her which offered a degree of separation. I waited for her because I sensed there was a reason for my presence.

"I am entirely grateful for your shepherding of Ronald in this horrific case. He was given the task of providing you guidance and assistance. As you are aware, he is not thought of too highly by members of the department. Therefore, this was an opportunity for him to show his strengths and merits."

"He has provided adequate assistance and unique knowledge." There didn't seem to be any problem with stretching the truth a bit for the sake of a loving mother. But I waited for something else and I wasn't quite prepared for what it could be.

"Would you mind a personal question, Baron?"

"Not at all."

"Why is it you are not married?"

"I could ask the same of you."

"No man has ever, shall we say, enticed me enough to consider it."

"Ronald's father?"

I could see her clutch her glass and her lips purse and tense. The color in her eyes faded like clouds covering the moon.

"A rake. A rascal. He took advantage of me at a young age because I was naïve and open-minded. Certainly not the kind of man to whom a woman would wish to commit."

"What kind of man would that be?"

It was then her face became flush, not with embarrassment but with a kind of eagerness and enthusiasm and exuding a degree of heat. It was suddenly rather warm in the room much like a summer day at the beach.

"A man of strength and of compassion. One who has languished but has not let his suffering deter him from the right and true path. A man whose passions lie deep within his core and can only be unlocked by the right kind of woman."

For the briefest moment, I had the recollection of my first dalliance with a French girl in the war. Our patrol was assigned to reconnoiter the farmland two miles ahead of the forward position. Baron Witherspoon, who was a Corporal, led four of us until we made the main house by night fall. The owner had a wife, son, and two daughters, and allowed us to sleep in the barn. The elder daughter kept making eyes at me. It wasn't my intention to take advantage of the situation until I encountered her at the back of the house while I smoked a cigarette. At her relatively young age, she spoke with the same calm and measured tone Deanna

Roché now used and her intentions were every bit the same. This young girl had learned to do whatever was necessary for the benefit of her family. I could only wonder what Deanna was trying to accomplish.

"Can such a man possibly exist?"

"I think he does. And you, what kind of woman are you looking for?"

"I honestly don't know."

She laughed heartily, like we were watching a Chaplin movie, and drank her sherry in one swallow.

"To be honest, I think you do and you're just too much of a gentleman to say so."

"Perhaps it's one of my secrets."

"One of many, I'm sure."

Her hand came to rest on my knee. It reminded me of being at Miss Becky's house, sitting alongside the young lady I had selected for an evening of pleasure, preparing to retire to a bedroom upstairs and throw aside the gallantry of gentlemen and ladies. I had become so involved in this case I started to look upon a gracious woman as some kind of slattern who would wind up the victim of a remorseless killer. At the same time, I imagined what the killer himself saw as he looked at these women. I pictured the world before me through his eyes. The notion by itself did not scare me. The fact I could was the most frightening of all.

Chapter Thirty-Nine

The next morning, I awoke not knowing where I was again. There was a feeling of being disoriented, as though I were drunk, the surroundings although pleasant provided me with no bearings, no sense of place or time. I knew it wasn't the sherry but a more potent elixir. Something which I am certain most women possessed.

Although there was something alluring about Deanna Roché, she made me feel uncomfortable. Beth Handy was a sweet young girl with stars in her eyes. Heather Devore was worldly and seductive but ultimately not dangerous. Natalie Dixon was troubled and could have truly used my help. Yet none of them was much of a mystery in the end. Officer Roché's mother was neither a religious zealot nor a wanton vixen. She fell somewhere on the line in between.

I had been getting to the station house very early every morning, managing to stop at a diner that served a decent batch of biscuits and gravy. However, I had already slept well past the time I would be meeting up with Rackler so I decided to get breakfast anyway. Maybe changing my routine would give me greater clarity than I had so far.

It must have been my imagination but it felt like Officer Roché was waiting for me at the entrance. His pacing back and forth made it appear less of a coincidence. I figured he felt left out considering how important he was to me the first time around. Also, being shut out by his own mother must have made him feel less significant.

"Officer Roché," I said with a slight nod of my head.

"Officer Witherspoon, I thought of something relevant to your case."

"Certainly. Why don't you join me in the detectives' room and we can see what you've got." It was not going to take up much of my day to give Ronnie some consideration, especially in light of the fact he was even an outsider in his own department. As he was well versed in the evidence, he just might have something useful.

My pace was casual. I wanted to allow him the opportunity to speak, to step up to the plate, so to speak. He just looked straight ahead, lost in thought, nodding occasionally to himself.

"Ronnie, what happened to your father?"

"I never knew my father." The answer was sudden, delivered faster than a bullet.

"Your mother said he had taken advantage of her."

"My mother…" He stopped walking, still looking straight ahead, took a deep breath and then turned toward me. "My mother's past, from what I gather, was filled with frivolity and lack of discretion. My father probably took advantage of an opportunity and then never looked back."

"I'm sorry. I didn't mean to pry."

The face of sobriety softened into a relaxed boyish charm.

"Not at all. She has changed greatly. She places a

great deal of faith in the teachings of Sister Celeste and is proud of my work."

"Your work?"

"Yes. On the police force."

I had no idea what he was referring to. He was an ordinary patrol officer, mostly looking for traffic violations and minor infractions. Perhaps Deanna felt his presence on the force gave him a measure of authority.

"I'm sure she's proud of you."

Rackler was getting annoyed at Ronnie's theory the killer was going after outsiders, those who didn't fit in with proper society and decent folks. Roché sounded more like an offspring of Sister Celeste. Twenty minutes in, Rackler turned back toward his files and folders. Ronnie became mildly annoyed by this but was pleased he still held my attention. I became aware of his hands, how they were like a conductor when discussing the killer but turned into clenched fists when explaining each of the victims and the possible reasons they were targeted. It was an elaborate theory but not grounded in any of the facts we had compiled.

A knock on the door interrupted the extended session. One of the duty officers informed me a gentleman named Montisse was looking for me. There was a bit of a pause before the use of the word 'gentleman' as though the officer were making a valiant effort to be courteous. I told the officer to escort him to the room. I looked back at Rackler who was equally surprised.

The big moustache covered his mouth completely. Even if he were to smile, it would be impossible to know although it was doubtful if this beast of a man would ever show such an emotion. Montisse looked at me first, his eyes squinting slightly, and then indignation looking over my shoulder at Rackler. His head turned quickly to see Ronnie. He stared at the young officer, probably recalling how easy it was to frighten him the first time we went in to Stankey's private club. Then Montisse's eyes widened before he finally looked back to me, perhaps showing more eagerness than he intended.

"Mr. Stankey wishes to speak with you."

I told Rackler to pull the file on Tangerine Smith including her autopsy report, thanked Officer Roché for his insightful feedback, and placed my cap firmly on my head. I stood up and straightened my uniform. This was going to be official business.

It was evident Montisse provided Carson Stankey with support of many means and would remain silent for the most part. But the look on his face as he drove us from the downtown building across the river into Delano was one of desperate recollection. He was not the kind of man who paid attention to anything other than what might harm Carson Stankey. Yet there was something more significant stuck inside his head.

When we got to the club, we went immediately to the small room behind the curtain. I knew I had nothing to fear because there was an understanding between myself and Stankey. I had a job to do and he had a business to run. The goal was to prevent these two notions from continuing to cross paths. Finding this killer would restore the natural order within Delano.

Stankey probably thought Montisse would draw the curtain aside and leave after I had been seated. He unexpectedly stayed, walked over to Stankey, and conversed quietly with him. Stankey looked at me, and then continued to listen to Montisse. The only thing I could hear clearly was Stankey asking "Are you sure?" Stankey nodded and Montisse left.

"Why did you send for me?" I asked bluntly.

"Do you know the preacher Sister Celeste?"

"Yes. I spoke with her at length the last time she was here."

"Are you aware of how many of her former disciples work for me?" My silence pleased him because he knew something I didn't. "I'm sure it works both ways."

"Do they know something useful?"

"They know which ones are the most devout, the most righteous." Stankey smiled. He used those terms not out of deference or respect but to mock. I felt it was prudent to let him know where we were at with the investigation.

"We considered a killer with a similar kind of agenda. Forced repentance or an act of contrition."

"*Deus meus, ex toto corde poenitet me omnium meorum peccatorum, eaque detestor, quia peccando, non solum poenas a Te iuste statutas promeritus sum, sed praesertim quia offendi Te, summum bonum, ac dignum qui super omnia diligaris. Ideo firmiter propono, adiuvante gratia Tua, de cetero me non peccaturum peccandique occasiones proximas fugiturum.* Amen."

His recital of the Act of Contrition surprised me. The irony of the pimp who knew Latin made me wonder about all the men and women who went to church on a regular basis and spoke the words without anything in their hearts.

"Who is truly the righteous and devout, Stankey?"

"I was an altar boy once." It was my turn to smile. "However, what is more important is Montisse recalled something which could be even more useful to you."

I was told what it was plaguing the mind of the man with the heavy moustache. When I realized what he remembered, everything started to make more sense. Now was the hour to draw the man out of the shadows.

Chapter Forty

Montisse drove me back in silence, his eyes squinting in some kind of deep contemplation, the likes of which seemed unusual to me at the time. I never really considered what kind of man he really might have been. I knew he was not as talkative as Stankey who liked to hear the sound of his own voice. But Montisse surprised me when we got back to the station.

"The scars. Have they changed you?"

I wasn't sure exactly what he meant but I answered as best as I could.

"I was a different person before."

"And you changed?" I nodded. "For the better?"

"I just changed. I don't have the right to say better or worse. I suppose it's for others to judge." I started to leave the car but he reached out to touch my arm, not grab so much as get my attention.

"Be careful about letting others judge you. They don't know you as well as you know yourself."

Perhaps he was talking about himself, the brusque man with the moustache hiding his face. Maybe he was trying to hide. Then again, so was I. We all had secrets.

Ronnie Roché was no longer in the detectives' room. Neither was anyone else except for Rackler. I looked around suspiciously making sure no one would come in and then closed the door behind me. Rackler stopped what he was doing and looked at me like I was a suspect.

"Take a look again at all the victims. Tell me someone you think might be next or might make a good target."

"What? I don't know any prostitutes and I'm certainly not a killer." I had approached him so quickly he took personal offense rather than consider himself as a detective.

"I need you to think like him. Who would you go after? What is he looking for? Whose sin needs to be repented?"

He shook his head in disbelief I was asking such a crazy question. He was being put on the spot and taken out of his comfort zone. This weakened him. Since Sells forced retirement, I no longer could rely on his balanced approach and experience. I had no one I could trust like Dave Morton. I needed Rackler to follow me on nothing more than blind faith. He started talking out loud, at first sounding like he was talking to himself.

"Ok, we've got a moral crusader, right? Prostitutes are sinful. A woman who gives drugs to an addict is sinful. We've got former sinners who are part of a revival…"

"Who probably lapsed and sinned again somehow," I added, trying to keep his thoughts on the right path.

"So, let's say they did. You got the dancer who was trading favors. I mean, you've got a lot of different women who could be a target."

"Assuming Carson Stankey keeps a closer eye on his women and Miss Becky does the same, who else would be draw his attention?"

I watched Rackler's eyebrows come together tight

and then lift up and apart, making the strangest movements I had ever seen.

"We got a burlesque house in town. I don't go for that stuff myself but I could see this guy getting upset over some of the performers." It was a new thread.

I roamed around the lobby of the Warren Theater until a short pasty-faced older gentleman with a lot of wrinkles identifying himself as Gregory Freedman, the manager, accosted me in an attempt to be controlling. My police badge sucked the wind out of him. I asked him who the lead performer was. He escorted me to the stage, close to the wings.

She moved gracefully, danced in a kind of slow motion, a prepared sequence she was going over to ensure it was correct. She wasn't tall but her long legs gave her a sense of height. Her hair was jet black and shiny, a bowl cut, and she stood, hand on hip, cigarette in a long black holder, appearing like a wealthy woman on her way to Miami for the winter. She turned as Mr. Freedman called her name. Her eyes were ice blue. Her face was mostly white, as though sunlight was not a preferred tonic. Her lips were moist and very red. I was introduced with my title and designation.

"I'm Jeanette Ross. To what do I owe the pleasure of a visit from the Wichita Police Department? Was there another complaint about nudity?"

"You perform nude?" I felt a smile starting to form on my face and quickly suppressed it.

"I give the illusion of performing nude."

"You know a lot about illusions?" I asked, trying desperately hard to be sly.

"Does Jennifer Rothstein from Baltimore, Maryland know a lot about illusions?"

"Your real name?" She nodded and finally a smile broke through. She started walking away, stopped for a moment and peered coyly over her shoulder, then continued. I followed her largely because of the promising look.

"When the legitimate theater did not prove viable, I changed my name and my act."

We wound up back stage and in front of a door with a big star and the words JEANETTE ROSS in painted gold lettering. Apparently, she sang and danced, sometimes with long scarves or fans like Sally Rand. She told bawdy jokes and could be sexy when needed or as tough as a drunken sailor on other occasions. As she described herself, she was a survivor.

"You still haven't told me why you're here." Her digression into her life story was dreamlike and now she brought me back to reality.

"You're familiar with the series of brutal killings over the last several months?"

"Yes."

"Well, I think you might be targeted, especially if I'm around."

"Then you better leave." She smiled like it was the punch line to a joke.

"I can't do that. I need to catch this guy."

"And you're going to let him stab me?"

"I won't let it happen."

"Are you sure?" There were no more jokes to tell. This wasn't the first show on Saturday night. I had brought the cruelty of the world into her freewheeling fun-loving venue and I felt sick by it. Regrettably, I had no other options.

"I just want to come and visit you periodically.

Here at the theater, maybe take you for coffee."

"Like a date?" She raised an eyebrow, like a suspicious Joan Crawford.

"I wouldn't be so presumptuous."

"You might try it some time."

She stared at me intensely, those blue eyes digging in deep to mine, looking past the scars, and using all her skills to figure out who I was behind the mask. I could see she was strong more than brave. For a brief moment, we were somewhere else, laughing, running, rolling around. She was different than Heather or Natalie. She could take care of herself but preferred to let someone else take care of her. The job temporarily fell on me. My voice was calm but my words were direct like a Sunday school teacher. I tried to not use the word 'bait' because I didn't want her to think she was just an object. The people, or more correctly the men, who came to see her shows, thought of her in such a fashion. I wasn't going to. I touched her softly on the arm before getting up and moving toward the door.

"Baron."

"Yes?"

"You'll tell me about the scars sometime."

I nodded and left.

It was important I focus on what needed to be done. Jeanette Ross was the ideal next target, and I knew I could lead the killer to her and be prepared for a possible attack. Being enthralled with her was going to cloud my judgment when the time was near.

When I got back, I was expecting to advise Rackler of my plan. Captain Merton was there in the detectives' office, Rackler standing behind him, hands clasped together, head slightly bowed as though he were paying his respects.

"Officer Witherspoon. Detective Rackler has advised me you have an interesting theory."

I was a little bothered Rackler had gone to his supervisors after I laid out my ideas, indicating to him it was only speculation and we would need to put a plan into action to see if we could draw the suspect out. Perhaps it was the pressure, political or otherwise, that made him disclose what we discussed. For all I know, he may have been reporting to them directly this entire time in hopes of some consideration if the case were solved. For Rackler, it was never about public service but how the public could serve him.

"It's just a theory, sir." He stood stock still, not blinking, a block of stone waiting to be carved. He wanted to hear from me what he had already been told. "I think the killer is Officer Ronald Roché."

Chapter Forty-One

Merton's eyes beamed as wide as saucers. With his lower jaw slack, he was ready to catch flies. I figured Rackler felt obligated to let his superiors know the score but I had overestimated his ability to understand completely everything I had outlined. Maybe he didn't say anything at all to Captain Merton. The point was now there was something definitive to deal with.

"Were you aware his mother was assaulted when she was younger?" Merton simply shook his head. "Well, the result was a pregnancy and the child was Officer Roché. The birth certificate does not list a father."

"How do you know all this?"

I smiled broadly. I wasn't the scarred man with a past. I was the cop in charge.

"I did a great deal of research using several sources which is something your detectives should have been doing all along." I made sure to not look at Rackler directly. Raising my voice slightly made everyone aware of how I felt. "There are plenty of resources available which were completely overlooked. Who knows how many women could have been saved earlier?" I caught a tense look from Rackler out of the corner of my eye. "Apparently Mrs. Roché's father was well off and allowed her to live at home and raise the child. His own wife had died several years earlier."

"What's all this got to do with Ronnie?" Rackler let me know by his tone how upset he was. All he was going to wind up doing was proving he was more fit to be a trash collector.

"The father was extremely religious and instilled the same in his daughter, basically forcing her to repent. We've got church records on this, baptisms, and other rituals. But he was mean to his grandson according to several of Ronnie's teachers I was able to track down. So, you have a wayward woman who got pregnant, was forced to repent, becomes a religious zealot but still wants to be naughty. And you've got a child who sees the bad girl got away with it. He doesn't see any sort of repentance. Nothing real, anyway. He becomes a cop in the hope he can clean up the bad elements. All he winds up doing is menial jobs and never gets a chance to be a true crusader."

"And from there he becomes a murderer." Merton didn't say it like a question but his words didn't have a lot of force behind them. It was almost as though he were reciting lines, trying to memorize them to explain to someone else who was equally inept.

"I don't know. Like I said, it's just a theory."

"How do we prove this?" Rackler finally sounded like he was onboard or, at the very least, willing to run with this idea considering there was nothing else. Anything as long as the killer was caught and he could stick a feather in his cap.

"Any time he has been assigned to me, he's followed me around like I'm his big brother. Maybe I'm the father he never had. I can't tell. I figure if I get close to someone he thinks is a harlot or a sinner, he might do something to, well, protect me."

"Protect you? From what?" Captain Merton was the type of cop who looked at photos and reports. This kind of thinking was beyond his capability. I began to consider it was beyond most people and kept wondering how it was I could get into the mind of this killer. A scary notion until I realized such a person was hiding behind their own mask, appearing like an average Joe, while being someone completely different inside. It was something I could relate to considering I had done it for twenty years.

"Protect me from sin."

I told them about Jeanette Ross and how I would meet her now and again and how I would need two detectives beside Rackler to simply follow me, be on the lookout for someone in the shadows because it was how the killer operated, giving Ronnie enough time to see me with her. If he made a move, we could grab him.

"I don't know," Rackler said, retreating into doubt the way only someone with a small mind can do. "It seems like a whole lot of effort for a slim chance."

"You have any better ideas, John? Your former partner was willing to listen, willing to give anything a try."

Captain Merton stood up tall, straightened his jacket, and returned back into the image of a polished professional.

"Officer Witherspoon is correct. We need to make an effort and see if this…theory has any substance to it. I'll assign two detectives. But this plan goes no further than the four of you and myself. If this doesn't prove to be correct, we will have accused an officer of the Wichita Police Department of being a cold-blooded killer."

Merton walked out without looking back. His word was final, like a pharaoh of Egypt. This was far different than the only other case I worked on three years ago, the one where I couldn't have guessed sweet Natalie Dixon was on a rampage of revenge. I had no one else to assist me because I didn't want anyone to know what she had done and, more to the point, because I was starting to fall in love with her. It might have been I understood and possibly agreed with her motives. Now, another person who had gotten close to me had ulterior motives, and I wasn't sure I could save him either.

Detective Rackler ambled over to me, puffing his chest, acting like the prize bull at the state fair.

"So why is it you get to cozy up to the burlesque gal?"

I turned and faced him, my hot breath in his face, my eyes pinned to his, watching those eyes follow the lines all over my face.

"From now on, as long as I'm assigned to your department, you do everything I say, when I say it. You see, what's going to happen is we're going to catch this guy. You'll wind up the big hero and I head back to Ark City to live a quiet and cozy life. And all you have to do is keep your mouth shut and follow me on this one. Do you understand me?"

For just the slightest moment, I felt like I was wearing a silk suit and stomping the pavement on North LaSalle with the Market Street Gang and getting respect just from staring everyone down. It was different in the war. You had to fight not only to keep yourself alive but your brothers in arms as well. But Dion O'Banion, the leader of the North Side Gang and the guy who convinced Eric Kimble to fight the Hun and get out of the streets, taught us in the early days a hard look will hold anyone at bay. John Rackler may have been the toughest kid on his street but he was in the big city now going after a killer who had no reason to stop. If my getting close to him put him off, he was never going to make it as a detective. I knew he was fuming but the steam hadn't yet escaped from the kettle.

I left the detectives' room and headed for a barber shop to get a shave. I was going to the Warren Theater to meet a lady.

Chapter Forty-Two

There I stood at the crossroads wondering who I was and who I should be. A tough from the North Side. A war hero. A fake identity. A real cop. A detective pressed into service. A hopeful detective. One who entered the minds of killers and thought like them. Why? Maybe because it's who I was deep down. I certainly wasn't a husband, a father, a brother, an uncle, a homeowner, an exemplary church-going member of the community. I was Baron Witherspoon, a name, a cop, with some sense of community and absolutely no idea of where I was going.

There was certainly nothing like the Warren Theater in Ark City and nothing at all like Jeanette Ross. Not even the lace covered Mademoiselles during the war compared to the slinky and sultry dancing, covered with feathers and silk scarves. Perhaps she was really nude but probably not. Yet you would never know for sure.

What surprised me the most was her singing. I had only heard opera once or twice from Dr. Brenz when he played it on a phonograph. She didn't quite hit the highest notes. Instead she sounded more like a songbird, a kind of sweetness and gentility. It was almost like a mother singing a lullaby. While there were a few ornery gents who could do without the song, the majority of the audience seemed captivated.

At the end of the show, Mr. Freedman escorted me discreetly to Miss Ross' dressing room. It was there I saw her wearing a skintight outfit almost the color of her skin. This was the illusion she had referred to earlier. I counted on her to be able to continue the illusion.

"So, how does this work?" she asked eagerly, hands on her knees, leaning forward in anticipation. Perhaps in order to get through the potential horror of the situation, Jeanette thought of this as just another performance. If that worked for her, it was okay by me.

"I come to the show and take you out to a late supper. Or I meet you in the afternoon to go shopping or to lunch. I just need to be out in public with you to allow us to be seen."

"By who?"

"By him."

Her face took on a more serious appearance, the curve of her smile straightened but her brow tightened. I hoped she realized I meant something more than a man, something sick and evil and twisted. Perhaps such monstrosity was something she had never encountered before. She tried to lighten the mood.

"Aren't you worried about your reputation, Officer Witherspoon?"

"I don't have one, Miss Ross."

After a quick change into regular clothes, we went to dinner. She ordered a steak, rare, and I had a plate of spaghetti with meatballs. She ate like she was starving but I knew she was paid well for her work and could afford whatever her pleasures may have been. I wondered where all her energy came from. I had experienced her beauty, her wit, her charm, and her talent. I wasn't sure if I was getting to know the real Jeanette Ross or a character in a stage show.

"Can I ask you a question?" I nodded. "Do you like being a cop?"

"Yes. I do."

"Why?"

It struck me because I had never been asked the question before and didn't have an answer right off the top of my head. I knew for going on twenty years being a beat cop in Ark City was what my life had become and gave me a sense of purpose. For the life of me, I just couldn't figure out why.

"It gives me something to do."

She wiped her lips gently with the napkin, pushed the now empty plate forward, and leaned in.

"I have a feeling there's a lot more to you than you're letting on. And since we're going to be spending quite some time together, I'm going to find out what that is."

What if she found out everything? I wondered. Would she be scared or angry? Would there be a sense of excitement? I was almost to the point of just telling her because I was getting tired. At times the uncertainty felt like heavy stones pressing down on me. For now, I'd allow her to enjoy her game.

Over the next few days, I made sure to provide Officer Roché access to the detectives' room anytime he wished, if he had more theories or further information to pass along. We wanted to allow him to be part of the investigation and close enough to me to be aware of my relationship with Jeanette.

One afternoon, Rackler and I were reviewing files. It was the same ones we had looked over countless times before. This time it was to make it appear we had a new lead or a new thought on the case. I yawned in the middle of a sentence.

"I'm sorry. I didn't get any breakfast this morning."

"Why don't you head out for lunch?" Rackler said, sounding friendlier and more accommodating than he ever had. Of course I knew it was an act. I looked up at the clock on the wall. Ronnie looked back and forth between me and Rackler.

"I guess I could go meet Jeanette. Afternoon rehearsals are done."

"Are you seeing her?"

"Well, kind of, I guess. After all, I'm going to be here in Wichita for a while and it's not often I get a chance to go out with someone like her. They don't have her type in Ark City."

Rackler laughed knowingly. Ronnie continued moving his head back and forth like some sort of wide-eyed bird. I patted him on the shoulder as I left. The point was to carry on like everything was normal and allow the other two detectives who were assigned to this case by Captain Merton to follow and report. I got back nearly two hours later meeting Rackler in another office to avoid Ronnie.

"He was following you two." Rackler pulled out a notebook. "Apparently he got to the theater before you. He put as good a tail on you as the dicks did on him. He left the outside of the restaurant you were at about fifteen minutes before you did. Detective Voth followed him back here to the station while Detective Montgomery waited on you."

"Just following me, huh? Seems like it's all we

have for now."

"It's something. It's more than we had."

"It doesn't prove anything. I'm going to have to push this thing more."

"How?"

"Start seeing her more like a suitor. Start talking about her in front of him. We need to get a response out of him. At this point, we have no idea how he may have encountered the other victims, what they might have said or done to get him to do what he did. Hell, for all I know, he just might be a puppy dog who's jealous of me."

It was a scary thought. If I was wrong I would be ruining this young man's reputation, his confidence, his whole career on the police force. It seemed to me Ronnie Roché had so little to begin with I didn't want to take everything away from him.

A few nights later, I was out late with Jeanette, she held onto my arm as though I were some European gentleman, the two of us laughing over a story she told. I don't know if Ronnie meant to allow us to see him but I called out to him. Bringing him to us was like sticking a dirty sock in his face. Jeanette represented the wayward side of sin, something not unlike his mother. And I, the representation of an older brother or perhaps a father, was wandering down a path of doom.

"Jeanette, this is Officer Ronald Roché, a bright young man on the force."

He tipped his cap and responded, "Ma'am." She wiggled like a worm on a hook but with far more oomph. There was a tight lipped look of contempt on his face, less anger and more like the beginnings of a fire and brimstone sermon.

"What brings you out tonight, Officer Roché?"

"I was looking for you. I recall someone from Sister Celeste's last meeting who might be a possible suspect."

"We'll discuss this in the morning." My tone was intentionally dismissive. I was attempting to hurt him as much as possible, especially in public and in front of Jeanette to goad him into eventually taking action. I was aware of Detectives Voth and Montgomery in the area and wanted them to witness everything as well.

Ronnie nodded toward me and walked off without looking at Jeanette.

"Is that him?" she asked.

"I think so. I don't know any more."

"He looks more the type to stomp his little feet in the ground and hold his breath until he turns blue."

I held her by the shoulders and turned her toward me.

"Don't underestimate him. There are dangers you know nothing about."

She leaned in toward the crook of my left arm, resting against it, while my right arm came up around her. I held her tightly and felt her heartbeat. Or maybe it was mine. I was starting to care about her just a little too much.

Chapter Forty-Three

Over the course of the next two weeks, there were more lunches and dinners and gatherings and walks and a trip to Jeanette's hotel room where she lived. Nothing happened other than her making me coffee and us really getting to know each other. It started to feel like a real relationship and not a police investigation in which she was the bait for a murderer.

Everything between us was easy, like floating on air. I didn't look upon her as something angelic nor as a fallen woman. She had a great deal of intelligence and was working hard to get somewhere in her field. She wasn't necessarily sure where but she had an admirable determination. I didn't feel lesser because of it. On the contrary, she actually motivated me.

Being around her was unlike Heather Devore or Natalie Dixon. Heather had the same sharp-as-nails demeanor and could take care of herself, up to a point. Natalie was radiant but hid a dark interior. Jeanette showed me a little of each and yet was someone completely different. I didn't feel as though I needed to protect her as long as we didn't have this case.

I was trusting Detectives Voth and Montgomery more than my own instincts and allowing Rackler, who I didn't have much faith in, to organize the reports and try to determine a pattern for Officer Roché's movements. Perhaps my thoughts were if I were more aware of my surroundings, Ronnie might not approach Jeanette or might even find someone else as a substitute for her, in essence killing the other girl as a symbol for Jeanette.

It got far too complicated in my mind I started to doubt my original theory. Perhaps even after all Ronnie Roché had gone through in his life this was all just a matter of him trying to prove himself in this world. I knew firsthand what it was like.

The second time I went over to Jeanette's apartment for coffee was late in the afternoon on a Wednesday. Rehearsals had completed and there was no show until Thursday night. She made a fresh pot of coffee and we sat across from each other at the table in the small kitchen. There was no dining room to speak of and only a sofa, stuffed chair, and a coffee table that passed itself off as a living area. For all the glamour of the entertainment business, her personal life was quiet and withdrawn.

"If you catch him, what happens then?" she asked.

"He'll go to trial. It's all up to the lawyers."

"I didn't mean that. I meant what happens to you?"

What she was really asking was what would happen to us. The real answer was I would go back to Arkansas City, Kansas where I lived and worked as a police officer and continue on my job for the remainder of my life and maybe make a difference to some people. By the same token, the answer might just as well have been I stayed here and worked on the Wichita Police Department so I could be closer to her. Where would that end up? Marriage? A house somewhere? The real Baron Witherspoon might already have settled down with Beth Handy and started a nice family, maybe even become a part of her dad's business. He might never have become a police officer. No matter what name I used, the man I was now was lost in what appeared to be a Kansas twister, spinning around and not knowing where he was going to land. Not so surprising when you consider Eliot Ness was much the same.

"What about you?" I asked as a way to avoid answering the question.

"I really would like to be a legitimate actress. I know I can do it. I just don't know if anyone will take me seriously after the so-called career I've had."

"You have to follow your dream."

"What's yours, Officer Witherspoon?"

She looked at me in a way no woman ever had before. She saw beyond and through my scars. Maybe she didn't know Eric Kimble but I felt her inside me as though to say "I don't care about the past, only the future."

The sad thing was I didn't believe in the future. In many ways, I was already dead, living on borrowed time, a second chance I had been trying to prove I had earned for the last twenty years. The world at large didn't need Eric Kimbles but more Baron Witherspoons. Unfortunately, they were stuck with me.

"I'm still looking for a dream," was the only thing I could respond. She reached across the table and touched my hand.

"Do you think I could be a part of it?"

I cleared my throat. It was less insensitive than pulling my hand away.

"Perhaps. But right now I've got to figure out a way to determine if Officer Roché might consider you a possible victim." Her eyes widened in surprise. The conversation had definitely gone in a different direction. It also made me think of another plan. "We're getting engaged." As wide as her eyes had been, they grew to the size of quarters while her mouth dropped open as well.

"Officer Witherspoon, I had no idea—"

"No. That's just the story. You represent something Ronnie believes is wrong. As long as we are seeing each other socially, he'll figure you are just a diversion while I'm on this case. But as soon as he sees you as a danger to me, he'll come to my rescue."

She squinted her eyes and her lips pursed. She was staring straight at me completely lost. I needed more than anything now to draw Ronnie out, force him to make a move and show me he was following a course of action intended to rid the city of evil and sin much in the way Sister Celeste had indicated, but not in the way she had intended. He wanted to prove to me he was worthy, and I was going to give him the opportunity.

"Well, I guess I'll find out what it's like to be engaged. I've never had the experience before. It will be my greatest performance yet."

I reached back across the table and held both of her hands in mine.

"I appreciate your willingness to help out in this case. We've spent a lot of time together, learned a lot about each other—"

"Not everything."

"No, not everything," I responded knowingly. "This is not how a couple grows together where one sends the other out into the dark. Perhaps when this is over we can spend some real time together. Maybe there is something for us. I don't know. But right now, I can't think about us. There is somebody out there brutally killing women. It doesn't matter some were prostitutes. Nobody deserves to die like that."

She nodded her head. Her eyes moistened but, knowing her, she was not going to let herself cry. She slowly removed her hands from mine, got up, and brought the coffee cups to the sink, cleaning them out and placing them on the dish rack. Her back to me, I watched as she lifted her head up and stood there for a moment. She turned toward me looking like she was ready to plow a field or chop down trees.

"Let's catch this guy." If nothing else, she was ready to complete the one task before going on to anything else.

Chapter Forty-Four

I was fairly confident of the plan but less so of Rackler's acting abilities. We were supposed to have what sounded like a normal conversation Ronnie Roché could overhear and perhaps be drawn into. Rackler sounded like he was reading straight from a script.

We were in the detectives' room when Officer Roché entered with a stack of files he had been asked to retrieve. Rackler and I were in the middle of a discussion.

"It's the strangest thing really. I never would have expected it. But it looks like Jeanette Ross and I are going to get married once I'm done with this case."

"Congratulations. I'm happy for you." Hollywood was definitely not calling on John Rackler.

"You're getting married to…Miss Ross?" Ronnie tried to make it sound as though he hadn't quite heard. Knowing him as I did, I could catch a slight warble in his voice like a child about to cry.

"Yes. I was just telling John about it. She's a very special lady."

"Are you moving here?" Now his voice sounded hopeful.

"No. We'll go back to Ark City."

"What will they think of her?" His tone changed again. Sharp yet direct. It was a question of importance for me to consider.

"What do you mean?"

"Well, folks down there aren't quite as open-minded as here in Wichita. I mean, after all, she is a fan dancer, right? Probably won't settle too well in Ark City, will it?"

I stood up and walked over to him, placed my hand on his shoulder like I was an older brother, and looked down at him with a smile of confidence.

"I don't think there's anything to worry about. People have accepted me when I returned from the war, being all scarred and looking like a monster. Given time, I became accepted."

He looked at my hand on his shoulder and then back at me.

"There's a difference between scars and sin. You'll be giving up your career."

He placed the files on the table and walked out. I walked softly over to the door and made out his shadow in the hallway. I returned to my seat near Rackler and spoke rather loudly and clearly.

"She's performing her last show on Friday. Then, no matter what happens with this case, I'm heading back home."

Later in the afternoon, I was summoned to Captain Merton's office. Rackler stepped out just as I was going in. It was strange how he didn't make any eye contact with me, rather just kept walking briskly past.

"Are you certain this will work?" Merton's entire intention was to determine if I knew what I was doing considering all his other options were limited.

"Assuming our assessment of Officer Roché is accurate, I have placed a specific timeline before him. This woman, as he sees it, is in a position to ruin my career. He will make certain it doesn't happen."

"I want to hear the details one more time."

"I'll drop off Miss Ross at the theater at her usual time and then leave. Detectives Rackler, Voth, and Montgomery will be strategically placed at the exits to the theater, most notably in the alley behind which is where Officer Roché will likely accost her upon her departure. This is similar to how Valeria Delsin was murdered. I will have left my hotel by the back entrance and made my way down to the theater as well. I will not be wearing my uniform to make it easier to blend in with pedestrians."

"And you're certain you'll be able to stop him before he—"

"Nothing will happen to her, sir."

He nodded and remained silent. I took it as my cue to leave.

I got in my car and drove, uncertain of where I was going. Detective Ed Sells understood and respected me but he was retired. Detective John Rackler was an incompetent fool who would wind up with all the glory. Officer Ronald Roché at first seemed like a put upon younger officer just looking for a chance but might wind up being a killer. His mother, Deanna Roché, was lost in a world of delusion somewhere between righteousness and damnation. I was alone in a big city without anyone I could trust or rely on. There was only one place to go.

Jeanette Ross answered the door in a silk robe. I couldn't tell if it was something she wore regularly or if she was expecting me to drop by. Her ice blue eyes had a cool and calm influence.

"Is this a social call?" She smiled.

"Well, we are engaged." I smiled back. She took a step back and opened the door wider. I walked in feeling like I had gone through the Battle of the Marne.

"Would you like a drink?" I nodded. She poured whiskey straight into a glass. I took a sip, then a bigger one.

"You're all set with the plan?"

"You escort me to the theater tomorrow. Your men are waiting at the back entrance. I do my regular show. I leave. Your guy tries to kill me. You grab him. Simple, right?"

She tried to sound relaxed but I had gotten to know her well enough to hear in her voice she was relying on her faith in me.

"Everything will be fine."

"I know. So, why are you really here?"

"I just came over to make him more upset. I'm sure he followed me." She started to walk over to the window. "Don't." She continued and stood there, pulling the curtain aside.

"Come over here," she said, looking over her shoulder, "and stand in back of me."

I stood close to her. The sky was thick with stars. Street lights lit up the night like a Broadway show. I looked down at her shoulder, her hips, her backside, a set of shimmering curves in silk. She smelled of lavender and honeysuckle and sweet freshness. She turned around suddenly while I stared down. When I looked up, I saw her tongue swipe across the glossy redness of her lips.

"If you really want to make him upset, you should stay the night."

I turned and walked back toward the kitchen

counter and poured more whiskey. I needed to think but I came here to stop thinking, to just drop the mask and be somebody different for a while. She was making it too easy.

"I'll sleep on your couch."

She strutted toward me, everything swaying in perfect rhythm, a Rube Goldberg machine in which all the parts were designed for pleasure. She grabbed the glass from my hand and took a big swig before placing the glass on the counter.

"I want to know you'll protect me. I need to know I'm something more than cheese in a mousetrap. That won't happen by you sleeping on my couch."

She grabbed me by the lapels the same way she took my glass and drew me toward her. Our lips met, locked, melted against each other. My arms came up around her, a hand on the back of her head, the other on the small of her back. I was pressing her to me as closely as it was possible. I did everything I could to make Ronnie Roché envious and upset without him ever knowing about it.

Chapter Forty-Five

The little kitchen wasn't much but it was enough to cook fried eggs, bacon, and toast. Even the coffee smelled good. This was no Daisy Mae's and Jeanette certainly wasn't Dixie. She was a darn sight something else, something more.

My face pulsated. I couldn't figure if it was from all her kissing or just because I was getting older and this was going to happen according to Dr. Brenz. Maybe it was because I was excited and felt alive again. It was unfortunate I didn't allow myself to keep those thoughts more often. I just didn't want to believe in my own happiness.

She placed the plate in front of me, poured a cup of coffee, and refilled hers. She sat down opposite me with a big smile.

"What about you?" I asked.

"I had a roll with butter."

"Nothing more?"

"How do you think I keep this girlish figure?" Her smile was like the sun on a summer's day slowly melting away the ice in a glass of lemonade. It was so warm the ice didn't even mind melting into nothingness. I shoveled forkfuls of food into my mouth like a doughboy in basic training, then looked up to see her watching me. Not staring or judging, just watching. I placed my fork down on the plate, took a sip of coffee before putting the cup down, and then returned her gaze.

"Is this something you could get used to?" I really wanted to know what she was thinking but I didn't know her as well as I thought.

"I'm taking it for a spin around the block."

"You trust me, right?"

Her smile faded, and she had the look of a little girl who had just returned home from being lost and who never wanted to get lost again. I had to be her guardian angel. After it was over, then we could determine if I was to be more.

We planned that on Friday, today, I was not to have any contact with Detective Rackler or Captain Merton or even Officer Ronnie Roché. The point was to be alone and a possible target. I left Jeanette's apartment, went back to my hotel, took a bath and had a shave, and then put on clean clothes. I checked and cleaned my service revolver and made sure to wear a jacket where I could keep it in the side pocket. I went over this plan in my head several times, more than what was necessary. Ronnie Roché was not a physically imposing figure. It would be easy to subdue him. Yet there were so many things I was unsure of it made me doubt, even then, he was the killer.

An alarming thought occurred to me. What if Ronnie Roché was not the killer and the real killer was following me? What if all our attention was focused on Jeanette and the killer was planning his next move elsewhere? I did what I could to stop thinking those thoughts. I had considered everything from several angles. Either I was a hundred percent right or dead wrong.

I took to reading the newspaper to pass the time. It seemed the *Wichita Beacon* had more national news than the *Traveler* could muster. There was a piece in the gossip column about Eliot Ness involved with a fashion illustrator named Evaline Michelow and they were the talk of the town. After burning down Kingsbury Run and catching heck for it and then getting a divorce, Eliot looked to have come out clean as a whistle.

The first show of the evening was at 7:00 p.m. Jeanette liked to get to the theater two hours early. I picked her up at 4:30 p.m. She was dressed in a simple gown, not overly fancy but still elegant. She took me by the arm, and I escorted her to my car. We gazed at each other almost the entire time, stopping only to make our way down the steps without tripping over our feet.

We drove slowly and in silence. As she had told me before, she was going over her jokes and songs in her mind and retracing the dance steps and motion of her arms. It really was an impressive performance, the illusion of being completely nude behind those feathers. I was fortunate enough to have been able to see beyond the illusion.

I let her out of the car and gave her a peck on the cheek. I started to walk off. She grabbed me by the hands and pulled me close, her lips up to my ear.

"I've never been in love with anyone before. Is this what it feels like?" There was a slight trill in her voice.

"I guess we'll both find out together." I pulled away from her and watched her walk into the theater. Now was the time to trust Rackler, Voth, and Montgomery.

Each show was about ninety minutes. The first one

ended about 8:30 p.m. The performers got thirty
minutes to freshen up before the next show started at
9:00 p.m. Figuring Jeanette would remove her make-up
and change, I planned to meet her at the back entrance
by about 11:00 p.m. It would be six hours of doing
nothing but waiting. I would have to spend a good
portion of the time in the hotel just in case Ronnie was
watching me and wondering what I was doing. I'm sure
I realized all of this when we were putting this plan
together but it didn't hit me until now just how much
time had to pass in order to allow this thing play out. I
didn't want to take a nap and get some shut eye in case
I overslept.

In the lobby of the hotel, there was a newsstand. I
grabbed a copy of *Modern Screen* and *Popular
Detective*. I don't know what impulse caused me to
reach for those two until I realized each one reminded
me of Jeanette and myself. I sat in my room and
laughed to myself at the foolishness of both of these
rags.

The *Popular Detective* cover had a guy in a blue
suit shooting at another guy popping up through a
trapdoor in the floor, another guy dead at his feet, while
a third guy in suspenders and a white shirt had a mean
looking stevedore hook in his hands. Just for good
measure, a blonde dish was gagged and bound in what
looked like an upright coffin as though she were some
kind of floozy mummy.

On the other hand, *Modern Screen* featured Carole
Lombard with almost the same piercing blue eyes as
Jeanette wearing a classy yellow gown with the same
cleavage as Jeanette. She was sipping a drink through a
straw, her head lowered slightly, and looking up in a

kind of mischievous yet sexy way as though she knew what she wanted and how to get it. Going back and forth between these two made me realize how little the reading public knew of the real world.

Time passed as much as it could before I had to get out from the enclosure of the four walls of my room. I went to the coffee shop in the lobby and sat there for a while until I noticed the clock indicated it was 10:00 p.m. Leaving now, would allow me to get into a position to hopefully catch Ronnie before he tried anything.

Walking into the lobby, however, I saw something I wasn't prepared to deal with. It was Deanna Roché in a gown not quite unlike Carole Lombard's. She was dressed like a leopard waiting to pounce and I was the prey.

Chapter Forty-Six

There was no sense causing a scene in the lobby. It was probably not the best thing to do to bring her back to my room but I had limited options. There was still plenty of time for me to get to the theater. My gaze darted all around, primarily over her shoulder, feeling like a prisoner of war trying to escape.

"To what do I owe the pleasure, Mrs. Roché?" I realized the word 'pleasure' was not appropriate, given how she had been rather forward the last time I saw her.

"I must correct you, Baron. As I've never been married, it is Miss Roché. And I'm here to declare my intentions for you." I stared at her blankly not fully understanding what she was trying to say. Was she placing a bid on an item at auction? "Ronald has advised me you plan to marry a burlesque performer."

"Yes."

"She doesn't hold a candle to me. I have money and influence the likes of which she can only dream of."

"There's more to marriage than all that, Miss Roché."

"Well, if this is so, I have studied the Oriental and French techniques and am adept at a wide range of pleasures. The Ross girl is a harlot who is not worth a man of your integrity and strength."

I realized she wasn't putting in a bid so much as

applying for a job.

"Does Ronnie feel the same way?"

Her chin was pointed at me like a small caliber gun. Her nostrils flared. Her eyes widened and focused on me.

"He feels whatever way I tell him to feel."

I didn't need Dr. Brenz to tell me this woman was insane. She was torn between being a complete wanton harlot and the repentance instilled in her by her deep religious upbringing. She presented herself as upright and moral but deep down she wanted to be like all the prostitutes she had somehow caused Ronnie to hate. Without actually putting the knife in his hand, she encouraged Ronnie's actions by her attitudes and behavior. There was no doubt in my mind now he would be waiting in the alley for Jeanette. The point was for me to get there as well.

I walked toward the door, but she stepped in front of me. I tried to step to one side and then the other but she mirrored my moves. She reached out with both hands and grabbed my face trying to kiss me. I grabbed her wrists and pushed her away from me. She started hissing and panting like a feral cat, doing everything she could to grab me, not violently but in some dance of lust. She pulled at her dress, ripping it and exposing her breasts to me.

"Take me. You must take me. I'm the only one good enough for you."

It was never my intention to raise a hand to a woman but right now this beast was in my way. With a sweep of my arm, I pushed her shoulder and flung her down to the floor and left the room before she had a chance to get up.

The clock in the coffee shop showed 10:20 p.m. I rushed to my car and drove down Douglas Ave. stopping at several traffic lights and letting late night crowds pass in the crosswalk. I should have had more faith in the other detectives but I couldn't trust them to be where they needed to be. I finally managed to turn up Broadway but there were cars moving in both directions, revelers looking to extend their Friday night pleasure, the biggest crowd coming out of the Orpheum Theater at Second Street. It seemed like crossing a French forest with German artillery all around to go the additional six blocks. In the distance I could see a crowd was still milling about in front on the Warren. I parked on the street a block away and made my way behind buildings and into the alley.

I kept close to the buildings and walked slowly seeing the one lone light shining over the stage door. I knew where Rackler and Voth and Montgomery were supposed to be but I couldn't see anyone, which I supposed was a good thing but made me nervous all the same. The light was unable to reach just beyond the stage door to the north. There were shadows, like a quiet cave for someone to hide in. I expected the beast to be somewhere in there.

As I moved, I became aware of lights above me and moved away from them to stay in the shadows myself. The alley I was in ended at Murdock where I would have to cross the street and continue toward the theater. It was there I would be vulnerable, exposed, and out in the open.

The stage door opened and Jeanette stepped out. She stood there at the back entrance and under the light. I thought I heard a sound, like a large crate moving.

Suddenly, there was the sound of sirens. A fire truck barreled down from the east on Murdock, passed right in front of me, and blocked my view of the alley.

As it passed, I saw Jeanette struggle with a short figure in the dark. She wasn't like the others; she knew to expect him. I ran across the street, not considering another fire truck could come along at any moment.

I reached the alley on the other side. Jeanette had Ronnie's wrists in her hands, keeping the long sharp knife as far from her as she could. I ran like Jesse Owens, lowered my head, and struck him in the body. The impact of me rushing into him knocked Jeanette backward. There was a dull thud as she hit the door.

Ronnie and I fell together, me on top of him. He had the strength of a possessed fiend and pushed me off him easily. The look on his face was of a rabid dog, mouth and lips moist with spit and snot spewing from his nose. He gripped the knife tightly. I reached for my gun and held it at arm's length.

"Don't do it, kid."

We stood opposite each other like two wrestlers. Several sets of feet ran into the alley from all sides. Montgomery and Rackler came from the south, one on either side of the alley entrance: Voth from the north, panting and out of breath. The knife clanked to the ground. Rackler roughly forced Ronnie's arms behind his back and put him in handcuffs.

"That siren threw us off," Rackler said defiantly. "Glad you were able to stop him." John Rackler had his prize but he hadn't really earned it. His cold stare turned into a politician's smile and made me sick.

I helped Jeanette up. She threw her arms around me and squeezed. Her body shook uncontrollably as though struck by lightning. It was then she started to cry. Her tears dampened by shoulder. It felt like I was being baptized.

Chapter Forty-Seven

Everybody has secrets. Jake Hickey. Chief Taylor. Natalie Dixon. Ronnie Roché. Yes, even me. They're like demons living inside, wrapping their claws around your soul. They guide you when you want to go elsewhere. They drain the words from your mouth when you wish to speak. They force you to think you are not who you think you are, who you claim you are, who you want to be.

I'm sure Dr. Brenz would be able to use his books to explain what had happened to Ronnie, how he had become the monster he was, and what if anything could be done for him. None of it mattered to me. I expected to find some large dark and scary beast. Instead, there was nothing more than a disturbed boy. It turned out to be the scariest thing of all.

Jeanette went to the hospital to be checked over. She insisted upon leaving, telling the doctor she had a show on Saturday night and offering him tickets. I, on the other hand, drank what little I had left of the bottle I brought with me. For the first time in a while, I was lonely.

The patrolman who came to my hotel on Monday morning escorted me to the mayor's office. He was quite impressed with me and honored to have been given such an assignment. He figured there would be some sort of medal or award. There shouldn't be anything special for just doing your job.

Dark wood walls surrounded a desk large enough to sleep on. Mayor Elmer R. Corn sat comfortably in a large leather chair behind it, looking more like a banker who was deciding about a loan application. On either side of him stood Chief Bowery and Captain Merton. They were wearing their dress uniforms and stood at attention. This appeared to be an official meeting. I wish I had known because I would have stood taller.

"The city of Wichita owes you a debt of gratitude, Officer Witherspoon." The mayor's lines seemed rehearsed. He was as bad an actor as Rackler. "You've helped us remove a menace from our streets."

"It was an honor, sir. I'm sure my chief will allow me sufficient time to testify at the trial if you'll just let him know when it's on the calendar." I was trying to be gracious and move this thing along and just leave. But as soon as I spoke, Bowery and Merton looked at each other, trying to figure out which one of them was going to respond. The mayor, for all his stiffness, continued.

"In the interests of public safety, the District Attorney has determined we will forego a trial in favor of Officer Roché's confinement at the Oneida Therapeutic Hospital." Without knowing anything about the facility, I gathered it was a place where lunatics were locked up in padded cells and given medications to keep them quiet for as long as was necessary.

"Public safety?" My voice cracked like I was still a teenager.

"The citizens of this city do not need to know a vicious murderer was a member of the police department." Merton's voice was firm and unyielding.

He was telling me facts, none of which were open for debate. "It would completely undermine our ongoing efforts to help this community grow and prosper."

"Do you understand our position, Officer Witherspoon?" Chief Bowery's voice was deeper than Merton's and echoed in the office. It had the subtle roar of a lion protecting its lair. The only thing he didn't show me was his fangs and claws. He didn't have to. I knew they were there.

I looked in turn at each of them. Their gaze fixed on me. There was no need for them to look at each other as they were all of the same mind.

"Completely," I responded, my words falling like a dull thud on the floor. I continued looking at them longer than I cared to until I realized they had nothing more to say and I no longer had any interest in listening. I walked toward the door.

"Officer Witherspoon." It was Merton's voice. I turned cautiously. "This is a police matter. Any discussion with unauthorized personnel will be considered obstruction of justice and subject to the appropriate legal action."

My eyes grew narrow. I stared at him hoping he would understand my disgust. It was then I realized they were no different than Deanie or George or former Councilman Hallett. I left as quickly as I could unless they wouldn't mind vomit on their rug.

Right then, my only solace was the woman who had demanded my protection, needed to know she would be safe with me. She was someone I wanted to get to know better. The knock on the door was answered quickly. She wore a white sun dress with flowers at the hem. Her hair was up but she wasn't made up like she was when she performed. It was the hug she gave me that caused doubt.

She offered me coffee but I declined. We sat at the same small dining table, holding hands as we had done so very recently.

"A little while back, I had gotten an offer from an old friend of mine, Charlotte Entin. She runs a big theater in San Francisco in the Tenderloin. I didn't think much of the offer at the time."

"But now you do." I didn't have to ask.

"Well, San Francisco is much bigger than Wichita. Hey, it might not be the legitimate theater—" Her voice trailed off. Maybe it was coming face to face with evil as opposed to a couple of drunks or too much reality for a person whose life is immersed in fantasy.

"Sure. It's a great opportunity." I tried to sound upbeat and encouraging. I wasn't sure how successful I was. I hadn't trained to be an actor.

She squeezed my hands tighter. "Why don't you come with me? Get away from all this."

I pulled my hands away slowly. "I can't." There was nothing more to say. How could I explain to her my life was not only here in Kansas but immersed in a small town that had embraced me, needed me? What kind of life could we have together, here or in California? I woke up from a pleasant dream and knew I had to put my feet back on the floor.

I got up to leave and she hugged me hard, almost cracking my ribs. The painful truth was we didn't fit in each other's world. After the hug, I turned without looking at her and left, closing the door behind me, and letting each of us continue down the paths we had created for ourselves.

It was approaching five o'clock when I made it back to Ark City. I knew Chief Richardson had left for the day so it wasn't necessary to check in and file a report. I also felt as though I would just fall asleep if I went straight home and likely sleep for a day and a half. There was only one place I could go to make me feel better: Daisy Mae's.

Dixie was slinging the hash behind the counter, saw me come in and grab a booth, and nodded in my direction. A young man in his twenties, well built like an athlete and with sandy blond hair, brought over a cup of coffee and a glass of water. He had a slight limp he tried hard to hide. It was few more minutes before she made her way over.

"Heard you was out of town on business." She always got straight to the point.

"You heard right."

"You back?"

"For good."

"You need a Salisbury steak with mashed potatoes and gravy."

"Yes, I do."

I ate the meal like I was a condemned man, enjoying every bite, sopping up the gravy with some white bread the young man brought over. After what seemed like the rest of the night, he came back to take my empty plate away. Dixie came back to refill my coffee.

"Who's the guy?"

"Name's Ralph Houseman. Come up from Oklahoma looking for work. Hired him a month ago. Busses the tables, does general maintenance. Good kid. Trustworthy." She saw I wasn't returning her smile as I had pretty much always done and wound up sitting in the booth opposite me. "What's on your mind, cowboy?"

"Do you have any secrets?"

"Sure I do."

"Like what?"

She let out a belly laugh, and the few people in the diner turned their heads in surprise.

"You silly fool. If I told you they wouldn't be secrets."

"Aren't you bothered by keeping them?"

"Nope." She said it almost too fast. "They're what make me who I am. I ain't about to give myself away to nobody. I'm not talking about love or nothing like that. There's a part of all of us we got hid deep down. It's what keeps us ticking. Take that away and we're nothing." She stood up and stared at me like a wise old schoolteacher. "You keep your secrets and I'll keep mine."

Eric Kimble appreciated her advice. So, too, did Baron Witherspoon.

A word from the author…

I studied film-making and creative writing at the University of Miami in the '80s, was involved in the Boston Poetry Scene in the '90s, and am a former president of the Kansas Writer's Association. My work has stretched from crime fiction to poetry, screen writing to experimental fiction.

I live in a one hundred plus year old Victorian home in Wichita, Kansas with my wife, Shelia, and Rupert, the tuxedo cat.

http://tikiman1962.wordpress.com

Thank you for purchasing
this publication of The Wild Rose Press, Inc.

If you enjoyed the story, we would appreciate your
letting others know by leaving a review.

For other wonderful stories,
please visit our on-line bookstore at
www.thewildrosepress.com.

For questions or more information
contact us at
info@thewildrosepress.com.

The Wild Rose Press, Inc.
www.thewildrosepress.com

Stay current with The Wild Rose Press, Inc.

Like us on Facebook

https://www.facebook.com/TheWildRosePress

And Follow us on Twitter
https://twitter.com/WildRosePress

Like a vaudeville show,

two large men entered on cue. The first one was younger, maybe in his mid thirties, built like a war horse but with a look of total anger and chaos, eyes that seemed to stare rather than see. There was something bullish about him, as though he were a runaway train, rolling over anybody and anything in its path. The man behind him was a good ten to fifteen years older than me, as big but seeming more like a large sack of flour with the same pale whiteness, looking like he had just awoken from a sound sleep. His steps fell heavy as he walked.

"This the guy?" blurted the younger man.

Roché pointed to the first and then the second man.

"Detective Rackler and Detective Sells, this is Officer Witherspoon from the Arkansas City…"

"I know who he is." Rackler's words cut like a bayonet through a soft body, making my outstretched hand seem useless. "I told the chief we don't need him."

Praise for H. B. Berlow

"H.B. Berlow writes with an extraordinary imagination expressed in a provocative crime thriller containing unforgettable characters."

~Dr. Bruce Lindsay,
Police commissioner (ret.),
Rochester, New Hampshire